The full moon was rising on a Saturday night in Kalamazoo City, the town that never sleeps. Bamboo, Kalamazoo City's hottest nightclub, was bouncing to the beat of the house band. Roxie, the lead singer, belted out their latest hits as teenagers jammed the dance floor. Servers swarmed around the room, hoisting trays heaped with the most delectable salmon, bass, tuna, and trout. There was simply no finer place to be.

Just above the packed dance floor was a dark pane of glass, and on the opposite side of that glass was Frank Pandini Jr.'s top-secret office. It was there that the city's richest businessman and its newly elected mayor could look down at his nightclub and watch who was coming in and out. This room also provided just enough privacy for activities Pandini wished to keep secret.

At that moment, Frank Pandini Jr. stood in front of a wall of video screens, engaged in just such an activity. The largest screen, in the center, showed a satellite map of the city and the waters that surrounded it. All of the other screens showed live video feeds from small cameras hidden in Pandini's other prime businesses. He could watch the local college football team lifting weights at Roar. Or he could peek at a couple canoodling over a romantic dinner at Black and White. Pandini's power and his vantage point gave him access to all the city's secrets. Most days he would stand in front of these monitors, beaming with pride at his success.

But today he was not smiling. He clenched his fists, and beads of sweat clung to the fur on his brow. He removed his trademark tuxedo jacket and draped it over the back of his chair. He rolled up his sleeves. He began to pace the office from one end to the other.

Bobby, Pandini's most trusted security guard,

cracked his massive knuckles. "You don't need to worry, boss," he said. "Everything is going as planned."

Irving Myers, Pandini's chief political strategist, wasn't even half Bobby's size, but his tone was just as tough. "*If* you-know-who is back—and that's a big *if*—it isn't anything we can't handle. We got you into the mayor's office, didn't we?"

Pandini paced even faster. "You don't know what he's capable of," he growled. "You don't know what he KNOWS. He could ruin everything we've built."

"You're the most powerful creature in the city," said Bobby. "There's nothing and nobody you can't stop."

"I'm so close," whispered Pandini. "So close to doing everything I set out to accomplish."

Bobby grinned. "Starting with the Platypus Police Squad."

Pandini nodded. "Every time I see a badge or hear a siren it is a reminder of what they did to my father, to my family."

Bobby and Irving had heard this all before. They knew their boss had to let off some steam.

Pandini continued. "My father built this town. He brought in the money and jobs that put Kalamazoo City on the map. He planted the seeds for these skyscrapers we see around us. So he bent a few laws here and there. This city would be *nothing* without him. A disaster. Abandoned. But does he get any credit? No. Instead he is remembered as a scourge, while Lieutenant Dailey has been elevated to sainthood in the memories of everyone who has benefited from my father's work, and his old partner, Corey O'Malley, is a celebrated veteran of the squad. And then there's that other detective—Rick Zengo, Lieutenant Dailey's

own grandson—who has been sticking his dumb duckbill into my business since the day he was given his boomerang."

"Someday we'll see that boomerang mounted, boss," Bobby said. "On your trophy wall."

"We'll mount his tail too," said Myers.

The map of Kalamazoo City began to beep. Pandini spun around to the center monitor. A tiny dot blinked offshore. It picked up speed as it inched closer and closer to the bay.

Pandini's eyes widened. "Now, what might that be?" he whispered hoarsely.

Two teenagers approached the docks on the south side of town, hand in hand.

"I don't know about this, Blake. It's pretty sketchy down here at night." Vanessa O'Malley clenched her boyfriend's paw tightly.

"Sweetie, it'll be fine," reassured Blake. "We'll get the best view of the full moon from down here. Besides, if any thugs try anything, I'll protect us." Blake put up his fists.

"Right," laughed Vanessa, rolling her eyes. "My hero."

They stepped toward the edge of the rickety dock. The wooden boards creaked beneath their feet, loud in the quiet night.

Vanessa turned her eyes to the choppy waters, where the reflection of the moon and stars sparkled before them. She gaped in awe. The night sky looked nothing like this from her bedroom window. This was like a light show.

"It's the last full moon before graduation," said Blake.

"Oh stop it," giggled Vanessa. "You're so dramatic."

"Just romantic," said Blake as he kissed her on the top of her head.

"Here, let's take a pic," said Vanessa. She pulled out her phone and extended her arm, pointing the lens back at them. They put their heads together as she hit the photo button.

That's when Vanessa heard a rumble. She looked at her boyfriend's stomach.

"Um . . . aren't you going to say 'excuse me'?"

"That wasn't me," he said.

They heard the rumble again, this time louder and out in the water.

"What's going on?" Vanessa asked. The ground began to tremble.

"I don't know," said Blake, his voice shaking. "But I think we should get out of here!"

Waves began to roll, breaking up the flicker of moonlight on the water. Blake and Vanessa turned to run. A dark shadow rose from the waters behind them, its horn piercing the night sky. It crashed onto the dock, sending shards of wood flying. Vanessa clutched her boyfriend's paw in one hand and her phone in the other as she bolted along the collapsing dock and dove headlong onto solid ground.

Vanessa turned and caught a glimpse of the creature just before it slipped back beneath the waves. It bellowed, an awful, pained roar.

The narwhal was back in Kalamazoo City.

Jarrett J. Krosoczka

PLATYPUS POLICE SQUAD

NEVER SAY NARWHAL

WALDEN POND PRESS

An Imprint of HarperCollins*Publishers*

MULLIGAN'S

TODAY'S SPECIALS:

Library of Congress Control Number: 2015956264
ISBN 978-0-06-207170-5

16 17 18 19 20 CG/RRDH 10 9 8 7 6 5 4 3 2 1
❖
First Edition

MULLIGAN'S, 10:58 P.M.

Detective Rick Zengo stared at the coffee in front of him. He usually kept himself sharp with a warm mug of hot chocolate, but these long shifts that the new crew in City Hall had him working were taking it out of him. He needed the caffeine just to stay awake. And besides, he was no longer a rookie on the Platypus Police Squad, no longer living with his parents in the home where he grew up. It was about time he started drinking something that didn't include marshmallows.

He grabbed five sugar packets, ripped them open,

1

and poured the contents into his mug.

His partner, Detective Corey O'Malley, looked up from his phone. "Jeepers, kid. You might as well throw some candy bars in there while you're at it!" O'Malley tapped his coffee mug. "I take mine black. Not a drop of milk, not a grain of sugar. Puts fur on your chest!"

Zengo poured cream into his mug until it was full to the brim. "We can't all be as tough as you, old-timer." Zengo took an uncertain sip of the concoction. It wasn't hot chocolate, but it wasn't so bad either.

He and his partner were sharing a booth with Special Investigator Jo Cooper, who was scanning the newspaper headlines.

"What's the latest in that old rag?" asked O'Malley.

Cooper folded the paper and slapped it on the table. "Unemployment rates have plummeted. Littering is at an all-time low. The Sharks have won eleven straight." She shrugged her shoulders. "By all accounts, the Pandini era is the best the city has ever seen."

"'Scuse me, darlins," interrupted Brenda, their server. She balanced the plates of the cops' late-night orders on her trunk. "Apple pie for you . . ." She placed the plate in front of Zengo. "Onion rings for you"— a plate for Cooper—"and the Hot Dog Explosion for you." A pyramid of hot dogs plopped in front of O'Malley as the condiments oozed out of the buns. O'Malley licked his bill.

"This will help me forget about all the trouble with these newfangled phones Pandini's making us carry," grumbled O'Malley.

"We've had them for a week," said Zengo. "You still haven't gotten the hang of them yet?"

O'Malley pointed his phone at his partner. "They call these smartphones? Know what I call them?"

Zengo rolled his eyes. "Let me guess: dumb phones?"

"I call them . . . um, that's right. Dumb phones." O'Malley stuffed a dog in his bill.

"They're supposed to increase our productivity, help us handle a larger workload," said Cooper. "It's about keeping the city safer. I think mine is pretty useful."

"With all these extra shifts they've got us working, I'd say it was a good investment," said Zengo. "Plus, you have to admit they're pretty cool. This voice-recognition software is state of the art."

"Malarkey!" cried O'Malley. "Watch this." He pressed a button on his phone, cleared his throat,

and said, "Call the station."

The screen swirled to life. *"Mall vacation. Here are some local malls perfect for a getaway."*

"NO! CALL THE STATION!" O'Malley shouted.

"Cod infestation. Searching . . . I have fifteen results from recent news feeds."

O'Malley slammed the phone down on the table. "See? It's a dumb phone! Totally dumb."

"You're mumbling," said Zengo. "Here, give it to me.

You just need to speak clearly." Zengo pressed the button and calmly said, "Call the station."

Once again, the computer voice sprang to life. *"Calling Platypus Police Squad headquarters."* Zengo ended the call before it could go through.

O'Malley reached into his breast pocket and pulled out his trusty old flip phone. "If I want to make a phone call, I'll use this—an actual phone! It only has one app, and it's amazing. Know what it does? *It makes phone calls.*"

"I think my grandma had one of those when I was a kid," said Zengo.

"Did you recently upgrade from two tin cans and a string?" asked Cooper.

The flip phone rang. O'Malley looked sideways at his colleagues and answered the call.

"Hi, sweetheart. Is everything okay?" O'Malley's face dropped. "A *what*? Where are you?"

Zengo's eyes met Cooper's—wondering.

"What were you doing down by the docks at night?" O'Malley's nostrils flared. He put his webbed hand over his face. "No, never mind. Stay put. I'm coming to pick you up."

O'Malley sprang up, knocking the hot dogs off his

plate. Zengo glanced at Cooper, who looked as worried as he did. It wasn't like O'Malley to get up from a full plate.

"It's Vanessa," O'Malley explained. "She and her boyfriend said the docks have been destroyed by a . . . Well, we'd better get down there. Sounds like we've caught a live one." O'Malley threw a few bills down on the table. "C'mon, let's go."

Zengo looked with regret at the remains of the slice of apple pie on his plate. He grabbed one last forkful and shoved it in his mouth before he threw on his jacket and followed his squad mates out the door.

PLATYPUS POLICE SQUAD HEADQUARTERS, 11:46 P.M.

Headquarters was as packed as usual on a Saturday night. Vanessa and Blake, wrapped in blankets, were huddled together at O'Malley's desk watching the action. Criminals being dragged in by weary officers, getting their mug shots taken, demanding their phone calls before being led to their cells. Vanessa looked at her father and imagined the characters he must have seen over the years.

Zengo brought over two cups filled with hot chocolate. Those packs of instant he kept in his drawer always came in handy. The aroma brought Zengo right back to the winter days when he sat at his mother's kitchen table, chilled from the cold but warmed by the hot chocolate she put in front of him.

"Here ya go, guys," he said. They gladly accepted. They still hadn't shaken the chill of the cold water. Zengo flipped open his notepad. "So tell me more about what you saw."

"It must have been the size of a building," said Blake, still stunned.

"It looked like it was hungry. Like it wanted to eat us." Vanessa shuddered. "Maybe it wanted revenge for all the fish we eat in Kalamazoo City."

"Hmm, I wouldn't bet on it," said Zengo. "I don't know that fish are smart enough to seek revenge."

"I still don't know what you two were doing down at the docks at that hour," shot O'Malley. His eyes locked with Blake's.

"Sir, it was my fault—" Blake began to explain.

"I'm not saying it wasn't," snapped O'Malley, wheeling toward his daughter. "But Vanessa, if I've told you once I've told you a hundred times, rule number one—"

"'Nothing good happens by the docks after the sun

10

goes down.' Dad, I know."

"You didn't happen to get a photo of the beast, did you?" asked Cooper.

"No, it all happened so quickly," said Blake.

"We turned and ran for our lives," said Vanessa. "But I actually did have my phone out at the time."

"Of course you did," said O'Malley. "That thing might as well be glued to your webbed hands."

Vanessa ignored him. "We had been taking pictures of the moon; you wouldn't believe the view from the docks. Here, see for yourself." Vanessa handed her phone over to Cooper. She tapped the photo icon, and Vanessa's photos filled the screen. Cooper swiped through them. "Cute selfies," she said.

Zengo couldn't help but look over Cooper's shoulder. "Hold up." He reached for the phone. "What's that?" Zengo pinched at the screen and zoomed in on a shadowy figure behind Vanessa and Blake.

"That's what attacked us," said Vanessa.

"That," said Cooper, "is a narwhal."

"AHA!"

Diaz and Lucinni, who must have been eavesdropping on the conversation from behind a partition, lumbered over to O'Malley's desk. "A narwhal?" taunted Diaz.

"Next thing you're going to tell me is that there was a leprechaun and a unicorn down by the docks too!" Lucinni smirked.

"Yeah, any pics of Bigfoot on that phone?"

"Laugh all you want, fellas," said Cooper, turning the phone around for O'Malley to see. He swallowed hard. There was no mistaking the tusk on the creature in the photo.

"Um . . . guys?" Blake asked. "What exactly is a nar-whal?"

"It's a whale with a large tusk that grows in the front of its head," said Cooper. "The tusk resembles that of a unicorn, but these animals aren't fictional." She gave Diaz and Lucinni a dismissive look.

Zengo glanced at his partner and was shocked by what he saw. O'Malley had gone silent. Clearly, this wasn't just some rogue marine mammal. Something about this narwhal was stirring his old partner up.

"Where have you BEEN?" screamed Plazinski as he stormed into the bullpen, the gate slamming behind him. "Zengo! O'Malley! You two were supposed to meet police officers downtown an *hour* ago. There was a bank robbery at Kalamazoo City Federal Savings!

Did you think that whoever did it was just going to wait nearby until it was convenient for you to start investigating?"

Diaz and Lucinni gave each other a nudge and a wink. It was hard to resist gloating whenever their rivals got scolded. Plazinski spun around. "What are you two clowns doing here? Didn't you get the message to report to the KC Coliseum? Somebody has been selling fake tickets to tonight's Sharks game."

Zengo scanned his phone. "Sarge, I don't have any messages here from you."

"I put them in your calendars. You should have gotten an alert!"

Zengo was already thumbing through his notifications and his calendar. "No, sir. There is nothing here." Zengo turned the phone's screen to Plazinski.

"Figure out your phone, rookie," Plazinski barked. He caught sight of Vanessa and Blake wrapped in blankets. "What's going on here, O'Malley? Visiting hours are over! In fact, they never started! Get them out of here!"

"Sergeant," started O'Malley, "Vanessa and Blake aren't visiting. They're giving us key eyewitness accounts."

14

"Of what?"

"Well . . . of a narwhal, sir." O'Malley clenched his jaw.

The color drained from Plazinski's bill. It was usually bright red with anger. Zengo had never seen the sergeant grow so pale.

"Narwhal?" The sergeant's voice shook. "You're *sure* about that?"

Just then, every phone line on Peggy's desk began to ring. "Platypus Police Squad. One moment. Platypus Police Squad. One moment." She couldn't pick up the phones fast enough. Peggy was hardly speedy on a good day, and the overtime seemed to be taking its toll on the aging turtle.

"The tusk is unmistakable." Cooper jumped in, handing Vanessa's phone to Plazinski. "I just wonder—what would a narwhal be doing down here, so far from the Arctic?"

Plazinski's eyes grew wide as he stared at the photo. He swallowed hard, looked directly at O'Malley, and said, "There hasn't been a narwhal sighting in Kalamazoo City for . . . er, in a long time."

"Excuse . . . me . . ." said Peggy. She handed a notepad to Sergeant Plazinski. "There's trouble . . . down . . . at . . . the . . ."

"Docks?" said Zengo.

"Yes." Peggy smiled appreciatively. "A cruise ship . . . ran . . . into . . . rocks . . . in the . . . shallows. It's . . . sinking."

Zengo looked at his phone. "On such a calm night? How could this have happened?"

"This is no accident," muttered Plazinski, looking right at O'Malley again. "It's happening. Again." The sergeant made a motion with his webbed hand for

everyone to gather closer. "I'm going to need all hands on deck."

Zengo threw on his jacket. Cooper checked the safety on her boomerang. O'Malley brushed the last crumbs of hot dog bun off his shirt.

"Peggy, dispatch every uniformed officer on the beat, and send in the EMTs. We want to make sure everyone on board gets safely to shore." Plazinski dashed out the front door toward his car. "C'mon, Cooper. You'll ride with me."

O'Malley kissed Vanessa on the forehead and handed her a few bucks. "Stay safe, sweetheart. Here's some cash for a cab. Make sure they take you straight home." O'Malley turned to leave.

"I love you, Dad," Vanessa said, stopping O'Malley in his tracks.

"I love you too, kiddo." He turned to Blake. "You get home safely too, all right? And stay away from the docks."

That was unexpected, thought Zengo as he followed his partner to their car. Ordinarily, O'Malley would have been pretty pleased at the idea of a gigantic sea creature swallowing his daughter's boyfriend.

KALAMAZOO CITY STREETS, 12:19 A.M.

O'Malley clutched the steering wheel of the squad car as it weaved in and out of traffic. Zengo was itching to finally get a chance to drive, but he knew better than to ask on a night like this. At least O'Malley let Zengo flip on the lights and siren as he pushed the gas pedal to the floor.

"What's your history with this narwhal character?" Zengo asked.

O'Malley looked at his partner sideways. There were no secrets between them, not anymore. Zengo needed to know what had O'Malley so spooked.

O'Malley expertly navigated their speeding squad car through a busy intersection. "Back when Pandini Sr. was running this town—from the back room of his gangster nightclub, not the mayor's office like his son—he had grand plans. Even grander than running Kalamazoo City. Pandini Sr. wanted the country. And he decided to start with the lakes, the rivers, the ocean. If Pandini controlled the waters, he controlled trade. He thought he could use that to create a crime ring that would stretch across the entire country. Communications, smuggling, you name it."

"But it didn't work," said Zengo.

"You probably know that our showdown with Pandini happened down by the docks. We intercepted a shipment of illegal fish he was ready to receive, caught that rat red-handed. Me and your grandfather, as well as a few other brave officers who Pandini hadn't bribed to turn a blind eye to his crime family. We arrested every member of Pandini Sr.'s team that night. Every member, except for one—a narwhal named Benny the Tusk. Benny had been Pandini's right-hand man in his waters operation. He disappeared that night, and we never heard from him again."

O'Malley took a right-hand turn onto Twenty-Fourth Street, where he met a huge traffic jam. Construction workers had closed the road down to one lane. O'Malley's PPS-issued phone chirped to life. *"A better route is available. Rerouting."*

"Nobody asked you!" barked O'Malley. He took his phone and threw it in the backseat.

Sheesh, thought Zengo. If that phone wanted to stick around, it had better learn not to mess with O'Malley while he was driving.

"So you think this is the same narwhal?" asked Zengo as they crawled forward.

"I hope not," said O'Malley. "If it is, we sure as heck have a big fish to fry."

"Mammal, you mean."

"Right you are."

O'Malley finally pulled into the docks and parked behind Plazinski's and Diaz's cars.

"Where have you been?" asked Plazinski as they got out and shut the doors. "And what were you doing coming up Twenty-Fourth? There was construction all over that road! Didn't you use the GPS on your new phone?"

"Uh, no . . . I've been driving this route for years, Sarge—"

"Use the phone, O'Malley," said Plazinski as he buttoned his suit coat.

"Yes, sir," O'Malley said sheepishly.

Diaz and Lucinni chuckled under their breath as they buttoned their coats and followed the sergeant. Cooper stepped out of the passenger side of Sergeant Plazinski's car. She nodded at Zengo and O'Malley.

They rounded the corner onto the docks, and the wreck of the sinking ship spread before them. A team of EMTs and uniformed officers was scrambling to rescue everybody clinging to what was left of the ship.

"Boys," said Cooper, "let's go fishing."

Officer Phillip Menendez stepped forward to brief Plazinski and his team. "What's the latest, Menendez?"

"The cruise ship isn't going to sail again." Officer Menendez nodded toward the vessel. "But thankfully all the passengers and the ship's crew are accounted for."

"That's some quick work, Officer," said Plazinski. "Well done."

"Thank you, sir."

Plazinski led his team past a group of shivering

passengers to get a closer look at the wreckage. The moon lit up the late-night sky, and spotlights aimed at the ship offered a better view of the damage.

Plazinski pulled a pair of binoculars out of his coat pocket and trained them on the gaping hole on the starboard side. He reached past Cooper and Diaz and offered the binoculars to O'Malley.

O'Malley took a long look. Zengo squinted at the ship over his partner's shoulder; he wanted to see what all the fuss was about.

Finally, O'Malley exhaled and brought the binoculars down. "What do you think, boss?" Zengo swiped the binoculars and took a look for himself.

"No way it was a rock that made a hole like that," said Plazinski.

Looking more closely at the hole, Zengo agreed. "Rocks would have ripped a hole far lower on the boat," he said.

"And the hole is much too clean to have been caused by a crash," said O'Malley. "This . . . could be the work of—"

A flash of light suddenly blinded all six monotremes.

"Mmm . . . now this would make a good headline,"

said a voice as Zengo's eyes adjusted to the darkness once more. "PLATYPUS POLICE SQUAD STUMPED AT MYSTERIOUS CRUISE SHIP SABOTAGE!"

When Zengo's vision came back into focus he looked down to see none other than Derek Dougherty, readying his camera to snap another picture.

"The PPS cannot comment on an ongoing investigation," snarled Plazinski, refusing to make eye contact with the annoying little news hawk.

"Sergeant, you see exactly what I see," said Derek, pointing at the ruined ship. "There's no way that that hole was an accident. I don't know what caused it, but I do know that someone—or some*thing*—sank that ship on purpose. And the readers of the *Kalamazoo Krier* will all know soon too."

Zengo got down on one knee and put his bill right in Derek's face. "Listen, pal. Why don't you let the detectives do their jobs? Printing a rumor like that could start a panic. When we have some hard facts, we'll let you know."

"Sorry, *rookie*, but I've got to get this story out now if I'm going to make the morning edition. I'm seeing a hole in the side of a cruise ship, and your crew here ain't giving me any answers. If you want to start coughing up some theories, though, I'll gladly hear them." Derek took out his notepad and pen and smirked triumphantly.

Zengo stood up and turned to walk away; as he did, though, he swung his tail and knocked the reporter to the ground.

"Please pardon my fellow detective," said Cooper as the rest of the detectives followed Zengo back toward the docks. "But you *were* a little too close to an active crime scene."

"You'll regret that, Detective Zengo!" Derek shouted after them.

Zengo and O'Malley stood apart from the rest of the squad as the last of the passengers were loaded into waiting ambulances.

"What do you make of all this?" Zengo asked. "The hole in the side of the ship . . . could that be the handi-work of a narwhal tusk? Could Benny the Tusk be back in Kalamazoo City?"

"One thing I can say for sure: not many narwhals

make their way to Kalamazoo City." O'Malley peered out onto the dark waters beyond the reach of the searchlights. "We're going to find out soon, one way or another."

CITY HALL, 9:29 A.M.

Pandini sat at his desk in City Hall, reading this morning's *Kalamazoo Krier* for the third time. Across the front page, the headlines read: SCARE AT SEA. Accompanying the article was a photo of Zengo and O'Malley looking on as the cruise ship slowly sank. The caption read, "Detectives Rick Zengo and Corey O'Malley of the Platypus Police Squad were befuddled and, once again, too late to catch the culprit." Pandini finally put the paper down, satisfied.

"What's it like out there, Bobby?" he asked.

His head of security, who stood by the door, said,

"Folks are freaking out, boss."

"Very good," Pandini said. "Very, very good."

Irving Myers opened the door to the mayor's office. "We're ready for you, Mr. Mayor."

Pandini folded the newspaper and placed it on his desk. "I'll never grow tired of hearing that, Irving." He took in a deep breath through his nostrils. "Ahhhh. It's a beautiful day, boys. It's a beautiful day." Pandini stood, straightened his tie, and walked toward the door. He passed a mirror and paused to smile. Perfect. He was ready.

Reporters packed the press room. Irving Myers took to the microphone before the assembled crowd. "Good morning, everybody. Please welcome the mayor of Kalamazoo City—Frank Pandini Jr.!"

Pandini stepped out from behind a curtain and

strode to the podium. He smiled and nodded to everyone. Every big-shot reporter in the city had come, plus a number Pandini recognized from other cities; the disaster at the docks had caught the attention of people far away, even past Walhalla.

"Thank you for coming on what is a very, very sad morning for Kalamazoo City," Pandini began. He paused for a moment and adjusted the microphone. "Last night, a cruise ship was attacked. It is my understanding that this attack was not made by a citizen of Kalamazoo City. I took it upon myself to arrange for my own investigation, which has been working all through the night. My sources tell me this crime was perpetrated by an enemy not of this *land*. No. While the investigations are still ongoing, all evidence points . . . to the sea. If there is a sea creature out to destroy our way of life, I, as your mayor, will stop at nothing to protect you. We are citizens of Kalamazoo City, and we do not get pushed around. One way or another, we will restore order, and you and your families will be safe." He paused for a moment and looked around the room with confidence. "I will now take a couple of questions before my emergency meeting with the City Council."

The crowd roared to life, calling out all at once. Pandini spotted Derek Dougherty sitting in the front row. Derek barely tried to get the mayor's attention—he merely raised a finger. Pandini smiled down. "Yes, Mr. Dougherty."

Derek stood up. "Yes, Derek Dougherty from the *Kalamazoo Krier*. What, if anything, is the Platypus Police Squad doing to curb this terror?"

"The platypuses that wear badges and protect this city are a very hardworking group," Pandini stated. "It's true, they have been dealing with a number of

public embarrassments over the last few months, but their workload has been a heavy one, and we are in their debt. The uniformed officers showed great courage at the docks last night, rescuing innocent civilians from peril. My investigative team will be providing the PPS with all the information they uncovered last night, and Sergeant Plazinski has assured me they have their top detectives working on this. They tell me they'll get to the bottom of this within the week, and I, for one, believe in them."

Rick Zengo watched Pandini's press conference from the television in the PPS break room. Cooper sat beside him, sipping coffee. It had been a long night, and there was no rest for the weary—they were required to report for duty early that morning. Zengo wore these long hours on his face; he hadn't gotten a full night's sleep since Pandini took office.

"'I, for one, believe in them.' Did you hear that?" asked Zengo. "What, nobody else does?"

"At least he's showing some confidence in us," Cooper observed.

"Well, he should, considering how many times we've saved his hide."

"And you can bet that's what he's doing right now," said O'Malley. He had just walked into the break room to fill his coffee mug too, wearing the same shirt and tie he had on the previous night. "Saving his own hide. He might sound supportive, but he's putting it all on us, publicly, to solve this one, and in a week no less!"

"And if the narwhal strikes again before we can catch him, Pandini will make sure everyone knows it was our fault," said Zengo.

"I thought Pandini was your pal now," said O'Malley, staring right at Zengo as he sipped his coffee.

"Yeah, right." Zengo sneered. He had been assigned to protect the mayor during the special election a few months back, but they weren't exactly friends. "I got to see up close how he runs things. He seems clean to me, but that doesn't mean he's not only in this for himself." Zengo looked up to the television screen. Pandini continued to field questions from the reporters. "He knows how to work a crowd, that's for sure."

"Politics. It's all one big show," said O'Malley.

Though Zengo couldn't say he ever really learned to trust the secretive panda while he was working for him, he definitely didn't regret his time there. A part of him might have even started to like the guy—at least, the guy that Pandini pretended to be while Zengo was around. But up there on the television, at that press conference, smoothly handling the press and subtly protecting himself from blame . . . Zengo wasn't sure what to think.

Plazinski stormed into the break room and turned the television off. "Why are you deadbeats ignoring my messages?"

Cooper, Zengo, and O'Malley looked to one another for answers. Cooper spoke up first. "Sir, what are you talking about?"

"Your phones! Don't you ever check your phones? I sent you alerts with the new messaging app!"

They all took out their phones. "I've got nothing from you, Sarge," said Zengo.

Plazinski just stared at his detectives. Zengo didn't like the look of the vein that began to bulge on his forehead.

"Well, we're here, what do you need us to do?" asked Cooper, changing the subject.

"You're going to get out there and find out who sunk that ship! Peggy can't keep up with all the calls she's getting—reports of a hulking creature in the waters around Kalamazoo City."

"The narwhal wouldn't be foolish enough to swim around in broad daylight, would he?" Zengo asked.

Plazinski's veins became more pronounced, and Zengo wished that he had kept that thought to himself. "Well, we will never know if my three top detectives are spending the day in the break room sipping lattes, now will we?" Plazinski handed a stack of paperwork to O'Malley. "These are the calls that came in this morning. I want every nook and cranny of the waterfronts examined, then start chasing down these leads."

"Ten-four," said Cooper. The three cops headed toward the door.

"Oh, and one more thing," said Plazinski. "I'm sure you all heard Mayor Pandini just now. If we don't wrap this up by the end of the week, we will all be hanging by our tails. I know it's been a rough few months, but please—don't mess this up."

Zengo nodded. The clock was ticking.

KALAMAZOO CITY DOCKS, 11:02 A.M.

Zengo surveyed the ruined dock and pondered his next move. His detective training taught him he should start gathering evidence. But with chaos in every direction, where to begin? He grabbed an evidence bag and headed for the nearest pile of shattered wood. Just as he reached the pile and grabbed a handful of chips, the weakened dock planks beneath his feet began to tremble and groan.

Yikes.

He reversed direction, walking quickly and carefully backwards until he stood on firm ground.

That was a close one.

He shuddered as he looked out at the water that he had nearly fallen into. It was vast and open—and wet. Rick Zengo had the courage of a lion except for one thing. He was terrified of going into water. He hadn't even stepped into so much as a wading pool since he was a pup. And he was not about to change that now.

Zengo decided to abandon evidence collecting for the moment. He studied the dock crew, who were using huge cranes to right the crippled cruise ship. Their job would have been all but impossible except that the water wasn't terribly deep where the ship had crashed.

Zengo slipped his smartphone out of his pocket. No messages. He looked at his signal bars. No service. He remembered hearing some complaints about the lousy cell phone reception near the docks. He hoped Plazinski wasn't trying to reach them. He lifted the phone to take a few photos of the activity.

"Do you need to be on your phone every second?" barked O'Malley, coming up behind him.

Zengo rolled his eyes. "Trying to check for messages from the sergeant," he replied.

"Humph. Thought you were playing some video

40

game or something," said O'Malley. He pointed to Zengo's evidence bag. "You find anything?"

"Not really." Zengo held out the bag full of wood chips. "Just these shards of wood. What about you?"

"Same here. Just pieces of this shredded dock."

"Why would Benny the Tusk want to destroy the dock or sink a cruise ship?" asked Zengo as Cooper joined them. "What's the motive here?"

"*Allegedly* Benny the Tusk," interrupted Cooper. "We don't have any hard evidence that points to Benny. Or to any narwhal, for that matter."

"But what about the photos?" said Zengo.

"Those photos were blurry," said Cooper. "It could have been any mammoth sea creature. . . . A fake tusk can't be terribly hard to come by."

The notion that the creature was a bogus narwhal hadn't occurred to Zengo. He began to consider even stranger possibilities. "Could it have been someone disguised as a narwhal? Like the kid in the panda costume last year?"

"It's a possibility," said O'Malley, tapping his bill.

"And what about all the eyewitness accounts?" asked Zengo. He pulled out the stack of notes that Peggy had taken from callers.

"Very few of their stories match up," said Cooper, taking the notes from Zengo and sifting through them as she had already done several times before. "We'll follow these leads, but every one of the calls came in after Derek Dougherty ran that article, putting all sorts of ideas into people's minds. I'm thinking we don't rely on any of these 'sightings' until we have firmer evidence to back them up."

"Let's ask forensics to analyze what we've found here," said O'Malley. "Maybe they can find some evidence of who—or what—did this."

As Zengo scanned the area, wondering if there was anything here they were missing, a warm breeze wafted past, carrying a familiar scent. It gave Zengo an idea.

"Corey," Zengo said, "is there a Frank's Franks nearby?"

"They just built a stand about a block west of here," said O'Malley. "You hungry too? I'm all for a break!"

"I know you'd never say no to a food break," said Zengo, patting his partner on the back, "but I was thinking about possible security footage. When I was working with Pandini I found out he puts high-end surveillance equipment into every one of his businesses—and that includes Frank's Franks."

"What are we waiting for?" said O'Malley, licking his bill. The detectives hustled down the block.

The little hot dog shack was nestled between tall buildings just beyond the docks. While Cooper and Zengo looked over the menu, O'Malley stepped up to the window and gave his usual order. "Three dogs with the works."

Zengo watched the teenage Frank's Franks employee collect all the toppings. He marveled as the kid

heaped the buns impossibly high. Zengo could never figure out how O'Malley managed to hold all that glop inside the bun while he ate it. Then again, considering the condition of most of his partner's uniform shirts, he mostly didn't.

"Don't forget the relish—third container over," said O'Malley. He turned to his partners. "It's kinda freaky how every Frank's Franks joint looks exactly the same." Zengo followed O'Malley's gaze up to the inside corner of the shack's interior. There it was: a security camera.

"Three dogs with the works," said the kid as he handed over a mess of a plate.

"Your first day on the job . . . ?"

"Andy, sir!"

"Andy," said O'Malley as he handed the kid a crisp ten-dollar bill. "Keep the change."

"Yessir, just started." Andy took the bills in his paw. "Thanks! My first tip!"

O'Malley took a giant bite out of his first dog. "Did you work the afternoon or evening shift yesterday?"

"I worked until close."

"Most Frank's Franks are open until late. What time did you close?"

Zengo studied Andy. He was looking a bit uneasy.

"Um . . . we stay open until ten on the weekends."

"So did you hear what happened a block down the road?" O'Malley pressed on.

"At the docks? Yeah. I heard the commotion, but I didn't know what it was until I saw that article online about the cruise ship. Pretty freaky."

"Did you see anything yourself, firsthand?" asked O'Malley.

"No, I had locked up by that time. I did what anybody with half a brain would do when I heard all the chaos—I ran!"

"This Frank's Franks stand . . . does it have any surveillance video we could check out?" asked Zengo.

"Sir, I really can't help you with that. I'm not allowed to do much but take your order."

It was worth a shot, thought Zengo. Pandini undoubtedly monitored all his surveillance videos in his secret office above Bamboo. The kid probably never got near the footage.

"Maybe I could help you, Detectives?" said a familiar voice.

Zengo, Cooper, and O'Malley spun around. There stood Frank Pandini Jr. He was flanked by his staff,

and a hungry mob of reporters wasn't far behind.

"Mr. Mayor, good afternoon," said O'Malley. "We were looking to get access to footage from the security camera here. . . ."

"Well of course I would gladly make that available to the Platypus Police Squad. The safety of the citizens of Kalamazoo City is my number one priority, and if that helps track down the perpetrator of the attack on the dock, we will all rest better." Pandini nodded to Irving Myers. "Please make sure they get what they need."

Just then, Derek Dougherty stepped forward, seemingly out of thin air. *Why is this guy always around?* Zengo thought.

"Would you mind giving me a few quotes on what you hope to find on those tapes, Detective Zengo?" He pushed his mini-recorder into Zengo's bill.

"I'd like to give you a few quotes about something—"

Pandini put a paw on Zengo's shoulder. "Rick, come speak with me for a moment."

Zengo clenched his fists, and his partner approached him. "Go ahead, kid," O'Malley whispered. "I've got this."

As O'Malley politely told Derek that the Platypus Police Squad had nothing new to announce at this time, Pandini escorted Zengo a few steps away from the group. He spoke again, in a hushed tone.

"I know that you guys are all doing your best, but we need to get to the bottom of this issue now. We *both know* what it might mean for Kalamazoo City."

He gave Zengo a hard look. *Was he thinking about Benny as well?* Zengo swallowed and nodded.

Pandini smiled. "Good. I'm counting on you, Rick." Pandini gave Rick's shoulder a pat and turned back to his entourage. "Let's all head down to the crime scene and see it for ourselves. You don't mind, do you, Detectives?" The mayor nodded to his employee running the hot dog stand. "The fine members of the

Platypus Police Squad have been doing some hard work, son. Please put their orders on my personal tab." With that Pandini smiled at the detectives and lumbered down the street to tour the destruction.

Derek stepped up to the counter. "I'll have a—"

"Not you, Dougherty." O'Malley nudged him out of the way and turned to Andy as Derek slinked away. "I'll take three more dogs, please. The works!"

Cooper, O'Malley, and Zengo sat at the Frank's Franks picnic bench. Zengo and Cooper were still working on their early lunches while O'Malley wiped his mouth after inhaling his second round of sloppy dogs.

Once more, Zengo checked his phone. He didn't

want to miss any more messages or calendar updates from Plazinski. But there were no new alerts. Probably spotty cell coverage here too. He switched over to his news feed. That at least was coming through.

"Ack!" Zengo almost choked on his hot dog. "Look at this!"

Cooper glanced at Zengo's phone. "The *Krier* website . . . and the headline reads . . ."

"KALAMAZOO CITY'S FINEST STUFF THEIR BILLS WHILE CITY IS UNDER ATTACK," Zengo finished for her. There was even a photo of O'Malley taking his order from Andy just a few minutes before.

"Malarkey!" said O'Malley, swiping Zengo's phone out of his webbed hand. The screen went blank. O'Malley pursed his bill and tapped at the screen. "Where did it go? Who could've written that and posted it already?"

"Dougherty, of course!" said Zengo. "That slimy little—"

"Let's not let it get under our fur," said Cooper. "Maybe it's best we stay away from the internet today."

Zengo took the phone back from O'Malley. He took a deep breath and slipped it into his pocket.

At that moment, O'Malley's flip phone chirped to

life. He answered the phone with a flick of his wrist. "O'Malley here."

Zengo could hear the voice of Karen, O'Malley's wife. "Corey, are you okay?"

O'Malley patted his stomach. "Well, I might need an antacid, but nothing out of the ordinary. . . ."

"I'm talking about the brawl at the Sharks game! Aren't you down at the stadium?"

"Um . . . no. Why would I be? We're over at the docks, clear across town."

"According to the email that just popped up on your computer, you're *supposed* to be at the Coliseum. City Hall is worried about rival fans dusting it up."

"Ah, criminy," grumbled O'Malley. He pulled out his smartphone, but there were no messages. "Shoot." He turned to Zengo and Cooper. "Did you guys get a message from Plazinski?"

They pulled out their phones, looked down to their screens. Nothing. They just shrugged their shoulders and shook their heads.

"Honey, I gotta go," said O'Malley. "Thanks. Love you. Bye." O'Malley closed his phone and threw it in his jacket pocket. "These darned dumb phones are gonna be the end of us!"

Just then, like popcorn popping, all three detectives' phones started vibrating and beeping repeatedly. Dozens of alerts blazed across their screens.

Zengo looked down in horror. There were no less than three voice mails from Plazinski. He placed his phone on speaker so they all could hear. Then he put his head down on the picnic table. "I'm almost too nervous to listen," he said.

Plazinski's voice came through so loudly, Zengo imagined his fist would come out of the phone receiver and start swinging.

"Why are you still at the docks? Why aren't you picking up your phones? Today is the big game at the Coliseum, and you know how rowdy those Sharks and Gators games can get—you should have been there an hour ago! Do you not look at your calendars? Do you not check your phones for messages? Why are taxpayers wasting money on such expensive phones if you fools don't use them?"

They didn't even wait to listen to the other two messages from Plazinski. They leaped into the squad car. O'Malley flipped on the siren, and they were off.

KALAMAZOO CITY COLISEUM, 12:13 P.M.

O'Malley put the pedal to the metal all the way across town. He took the last turn before the Coliseum on two wheels. But then, still a block away, he had to come screeching to a halt. The road was entirely blocked by a furious mob of fans. They were all shouting and waving their arms, right in the middle of the road.

It was not unheard of for Kalamazoo City Sharks and Walhalla Gators games to get a little rowdy. But nothing like this.

"The game hasn't even started yet!" said Cooper.

"We need to get out there," said O'Malley, throwing

the car into park right in the middle of the street. The detectives exited the squad car, grasping their boomerangs, as the people who weren't involved in the brawl quickly made their way toward the parking lots.

A pack of uniformed cops ran past the detectives. "If they're just getting here, that isn't good," said Zengo under his breath. He and his partners ran through the rabble like fish swimming upstream. Every few feet, hecklers yelled at the duck-billed detectives.

"It's about time you got here!"

"Pffft! Get yer head out from between yer tails and do yer jobs!"

These were the kinder words hurled at them.

By the time they arrived at the front gate of the Coliseum, the uniformed police officers had just about brought the brawl to an end. Max Pearson, the on-the-street reporter for Channel Five's Action News, was already there. He motioned for his camera operator to turn around as he spotted the approaching detectives.

"A few questions, if you don't mind," he said. "Why is the Platypus Police Squad only now getting onto the scene?"

"No comment," sneered O'Malley as he attempted to push past the camera.

Police officers held the fans of the two teams apart. As the few dozen brawlers on the Sharks side saw the PPS detectives approaching, they turned their rage on them.

"Where've ya been, flatfoots?"

"What a waste of the taxpayers' money! Hey, you! Old man! You've got mustard on your shirt!"

Max Pearson tapped O'Malley on the shoulder. "Detective, it does look like you have mustard dribbled down your shirt."

"OH, CRUDDLE STICKS!" yelled O'Malley.

The reporter reached and touched the stain. "By the look of this, I'd say this mustard is fresh."

"Hey, Officers!" shouted a loudmouth fan. "You gonna throw these Gator guttersnipes out of town for attacking us in front of our own stadium?"

"Us?" said a Gators fan. "*You're* the morons who started throwing punches!"

"Nice police department you've got here," said another Gators fan, laughing.

The Sharks fans surged toward O'Malley, and it was all the officers could do to hold them back. Zengo took a step toward them, but O'Malley put a paw on his back.

"Don't let any of this get to you, Rick. The public is angry, and they have every right to be. We weren't here. C'mon, let's just hang back and let the officers do their jobs."

"So we're just going to do nothing?" Zengo said.

"Nope," said Cooper. "Guys, keep your eyes peeled, see if you can't spot anything out of the ordinary in this crowd. I've never seen Sharks and Gators fans in a fight like this. Something smells fishy to me."

The three stood with their backs to the Coliseum and watched while the uniformed officers organized everyone into two lines so they could finally go into the stadium. The Sharks and Gators fans eyed one another suspiciously but didn't start fighting again. The entire time, the detectives observed everyone with eagle eyes.

Zengo's phone vibrated. *Plazinski again?* he thought. But it was a news alert from the *Kalamazoo Krier.* The headline on the lock screen read, PPS DETECTIVES STUFF FACES DURING COLISEUM CALAMITY.

"Cruddle sticks!" Zengo said. "Guys, I think we have a problem on our hands here."

He opened the article, which prominently featured the three detectives eating their complimentary hot dogs from Frank's Franks, right beside an image of the brawl in front of the Coliseum.

"Dougherty," Zengo said with gritted teeth. "How could he have been snapping photos in two places at once?"

Cooper had her own phone open and read the article out loud. "As a melee broke out at the Kalamazoo City Coliseum, three top detectives of the Platypus Police Squad stuffed their bills with street food. Sergeant Plazinski could not be reached for a statement, but police blotters report that the detectives, along with their uniformed peers, had been asked to report to the sports facility earlier in the day in the event things got rowdy between fans of the Kalamazoo City Sharks and Walhalla Gators prior to today's playoff game. Why would they ignore their superior's command? Are they lazy? Forgetful? Or have they just lost interest in protecting Kalamazoo City? They certainly haven't lost their interest in the famous hot dogs at Frank's Franks. Mayor Frank Pandini Jr. had this to say: 'I am disheartened to hear this latest report about yet another mistake made by the Platypus Police Squad. Our city is as strong as it has ever been, but there are still threats to its safety, both from inside and from outside. However, I believe in the PPS, just as I believe in every person in our fair city, and I believe they will

bounce back and be everything we know they can be.'"

Zengo pocketed his phone. "What's happening to us?" he asked his partners. "It seems like we can't get anything right these days."

"I don't know," said O'Malley. "But we need to get back on top of our game."

"We need to be even better than that," said Cooper as she glared at the photo of Derek Dougherty next to his article on the *Krier* website. "I think we have more than rowdy sports fans and fugitive sea creatures to watch out for."

KALAMAZOO CITY STREETS, 4:56 P.M.

"I feel like we're driving around in circles," said Cooper as she, Zengo, and O'Malley chased every lead in the stack of messages they had gotten from Peggy.

Zengo checked the PPSNAV app on his smartphone. This was a new tracking device designed to monitor every vehicle in the PPS. It was yet another new mandatory "productivity tool," courtesy of Sergeant Plazinski and Mayor Pandini. "You're right, Cooper," he said, showing her the record of their driving that day. It looked like a basket of curly fries.

"I wouldn't mind so much," said O'Malley, taking

yet another sharp right turn, "if any of these leads checked out."

"Agreed," said Cooper as she picked up one of the eyewitness reports. "Get this," she said, reading aloud. "Noreen McWhorter, age fifty-seven, out walking at 2300 last night."

"That's one hour before the events at the dock," said Zengo.

"Right," said Cooper. "McWhorter claims she spotted a hulking beast with a horn on the horizon."

"This could be legit," said O'Malley. "Let's go see her." He spun the wheel to the left, tightly rounding yet another corner.

"Not so fast," said Cooper. "The 'horn' she claims to have seen was a trumpet. Says she hates brass bands."

O'Malley shook his head; his shoulders slumped. "Next report," he said.

Zengo pulled one from his file. "This one is from Brixton Mathers, a custodian at Pandini Towers."

"Interesting," said Cooper. "Go on."

"He was taking a break last night, also at 2300," said Zengo. "During his break, he likes to go to the break room and look out across the city with his binoculars.

He said he saw something large and dark moving in the waters of the harbor."

"Best report yet, so far," said O'Malley, swerving to turn the vehicle in the direction of Pandini Towers.

Zengo studied the report. "Wait a second," he said. "Mathers describes what he saw as 'clearly a World War II–era submarine.'"

"Whaaat?" said O'Malley. "Sheesh. We've sure got a lousy bunch of eyewitnesses in this town."

"It's all because of that stupid photo in the newspaper," said Zengo. "It's got everyone seeing things in the harbor. Impossible to tell if anyone actually laid eyes on the narwhal attacking that cruise ship."

"This is nothing but a wild-goose chase," said Cooper.

"What have geese got to do with what happened down at the dock?" asked Zengo.

Cooper gave him a quizzical look. "I mean, everyone wants to be a part of this story. They're all just letting their imaginations run amok. Let's go back down to that Frank's Franks stand by the docks."

"But what about all this mess?" said Zengo, waving at the huge wad of eyewitness reports still uninvestigated.

"Those reports aren't going to tell us anything we don't already know," said Cooper. "The only way we're going to track down the narwhal is by getting our own eyes on him."

"But how?" asked Zengo.

Cooper's phone rang. "By getting our hands on that security footage. Hang on a second." She answered and listened to someone speaking on the other end. "Thanks, Lenny. Send them to my phone," she said, and hung up.

"Who was that?" asked O'Malley.

"An old pal with the feds," said Cooper. "They took over all outstanding Pandini Sr. cases after he was locked up decades ago. That includes anything related to Benny the Tusk. I convinced Lenny to issue us a search warrant on the suspicion that Benny was involved. Didn't even have to go through Plazinski."

O'Malley gave an admiring whistle. "Nice work, Jo," he said, turning the wheel once more to point the squad car toward the docks. "And right on time for an early late-afternoon snack."

Zengo's phone beeped. Another news alert. His bill went slack as he glanced at the screen. It was some sort of video made with news footage from the debacle at the Coliseum. The view count was staggering. Zengo couldn't resist—he pressed Play.

A synthesized beat poured out of the speakers.

"What are you watching?" O'Malley said.

They heard O'Malley's voice again—this time coming from the speakers, remixed over the beat.

"OH-OH-OH-OH CRUDDLE STICKS. Cruddle stickssss. Crud-crud-crud-crud cruddle STICKS!"

"What in the what?" shouted O'Malley.

"Looks like you're the latest internet sensation," said Zengo.

"Shut that off!" grumbled O'Malley, taking a turn more sharply than he probably needed to.

"As if we didn't already have enough problems," said Cooper. "We'd better solve this case soon. With all this bad publicity, I'm afraid it might be our last."

Even with the aid of the search warrant, Zengo thought they would have trouble securing the surveillance video. But Andy, working the afternoon shift today, took one look at the warrant on Cooper's phone, called his supervisor at Pandini headquarters, and then handed over a thumb drive.

"Thanks, man," said Cooper. She turned to her partners. "Zengo, do you want to check this out on the squad car's laptop?"

"Ten-four," said Zengo.

O'Malley shoved the last bite of a Frank's Everything Dog into his mouth, and he and Cooper ducked under the yellow caution tape and headed over to the damaged dock.

Zengo got into the squad car, opened the laptop, plugged in the thumb drive, and opened the video file. Grainy black-and-white footage filled the screen. The camera was positioned in the stand, so it caught

the back of the employee's head as well as the face
of anyone who strolled up looking for the special of
the day. Beyond that, you could see the street and, in
the distance, a sliver of the bay. Zengo leaned his seat
back, put the video on fast-forward, and kept his eyes
locked in on that small bit of water.

For a while there was no movement. Only the
occasional customer or pedestrian on the street.
The video featured that same kid sitting in the stand,
waiting for customers. Why would Pandini build a
Frank's Franks stand on this side of town, and keep
it open so late, if they weren't moving hot dogs? Was
it just a slow night? Zengo dutifully watched and
listened, with notepad in hand. The numbers on the

time stamp on the lower corner of the screen grew closer to ten p.m.

Finally, Blake and Vanessa came into the shot. They were walking past Frank's Franks toward the docks. Zengo sat forward in his chair. It wouldn't be long now before something happened. He slowed the playback down to normal speed and watched as Andy moved out from behind the counter. He was closing down the booth for the night. When the front shutter came down, Zengo would no longer have a view of the dock. He silently crossed his fingers that the camera would catch something before Andy dropped it.

That's when Zengo saw it—it was unmistakable. Emerging from the water was a narwhal, tusk and all. Zengo leaned in even closer for a better look, and that's when the shutter dropped and the screen went dark.

The sound kept rolling, though, and Zengo could hear a series of horrid, screeching roars. They sounded monstrous, like a horror movie creature on a rampage. The terrifying sounds were followed by the screams of Vanessa and Blake and the crashing sounds of Benny tearing the dock to bits. Then silence.

Zengo closed the laptop, jumped out of the cruiser, and ran down to the docks to share the news with his partners. He found O'Malley and Cooper talking to a worker high up on an electrical pole.

"Is this even legal?" barked O'Malley.

"Executive order from the mayor, sir," said the worker, who Zengo could see was installing something on the top of the pole.

"Get this, kid," said O'Malley to Zengo. "Pandini is installing cameras on every corner of the city."

"That might not be such a bad thing," said Zengo. He held up the thumb drive. "I think you guys are going to want to see this."

PLATYPUS POLICE SQUAD HEADQUARTERS, 6:06 P.M.

Mayor Pandini was standing behind the City Hall mayoral podium, doing what appeared to be one of his favorite things: talking to a room full of reporters who were hanging on his every word, as well as to the thousands of people watching live on the six o'clock news.

"In an effort to make Kalamazoo City a safer place for all its citizens, I have accepted a proposal from some of my most trusted advisors to install security cameras on nearly every corner of the city."

The reporters muttered and grumbled. Pandini

raised his voice to speak over them. "Now, I know this news will be alarming to some. I value the privacy of our citizens just as much as anyone. But if we are to remain vigilant in preventing more attacks like the mysterious one that has rocked Kalamazoo, we must have the tools to do so. A security camera from my business, the newest Frank's Franks located just on the outskirts of the south side piers, caught footage that confirms that we are under attack by a ferocious and vengeful narwhal—a violent criminal who will stop at nothing to destroy our peaceful city. This narwhal is none other than Benny the Tusk—one of Frank Pandini Sr.'s criminal partners who disappeared decades ago, but now, it seems, he has returned to continue the criminal work he began while working for my father."

Reporters' hands shot up, and they all started talking at once.

Back in the break room at Platypus Police Squad headquarters, a disgusted Rick Zengo watched Pandini answer questions.

"So, we get our hands on the Frank's Franks security footage, which Pandini has had in his possession for two days, and discover hard evidence that Benny the Tusk is the one who attacked the docks. And then, barely an hour later, Pandini decides to make this announcement." Zengo turned to his partners. "Does this seem suspicious to anyone else?"

On the television, Derek Dougherty stepped forward. Zengo clenched his fists as he watched Derek's lips twist in his trademark smarmy smirk.

"Yes, Mr. Mayor. Would you say that this new program is a direct reaction to the shortcomings of the Platypus Police Squad?"

"It would be wrong to characterize this move as such," said Pandini, his face blank. "Since you asked, though, I will say that while the PPS has struggled of late with keeping order in the city, they have done great work in the past—you may recall I was recently saved from an attack while under direct protection from the platypuses in blue. But that's not what's important here. What's important is that a beast from the deep is out to hurt our city once again. He remains at large. As your mayor, I am using all means available to me to put a solution in place that stops crime *before* it strikes. I sincerely hope that the Platypus Police Squad will be part of that solution, not a part of the problem."

In the break room, all the detectives groaned as one.

"I believe our best days lie ahead," continued Pandini. "And to put my full weight behind that statement, in spite of recent calamities, I have a surprise announcement. In just twenty-four hours, our fair city will be graced with a visit from the World Tour of the International Boating Association. Tomorrow at noon, some of the world's most luxurious vessels will glide into our waters. I had considered canceling this event because of the narwhal attacks, but I am confident now that we have the means to bring Benny the Tusk to justice. I have no doubt that between this surveillance program and the efforts of the Platypus Police Squad, we can ensure a peaceful day of family fun in and around the bay. Thank you, citizens of Kalamazoo City."

Zengo snapped the television off before he had to look at Pandini flashing his trademark grin to the audience once more. "There will be thousands of people on the docks tomorrow afternoon! How are we supposed to do our jobs?" The other members of the squad mumbled their agreement.

"Is there a problem, Detectives?" Sergeant Plazinski stood in the doorway with his arms crossed. "Because if you have something to say about protocol, you can say it right to my face."

Zengo spun around. "It's going to be a disaster, Sergeant. And how is it that we're just learning about this now? Didn't the mayor's office give you some advance warning about an event of this size?"

"You *have* known about the Sailboat Expo for a week, Detective," said Plazinski. "Though the announcement was a surprise to the general public, it has been listed in our official calendar for days. Check your phone!"

"I do check my phone!" yelled Zengo. "I look at it a million times a day! But I have never seen anything about this so-called World Tour Sailing thingy we are meant to provide security for. I'm beginning to doubt whether these precious phones you and the mayor outfitted us with even work!"

O'Malley was clearly frustrated himself. But he raised an eyebrow in warning at Zengo, who zipped his bill.

"Son," said Sergeant Plazinski, "I am going to strongly suggest you take a deep breath and reevaluate your attitude. A significant amount of the taxpayers' money went into purchasing these new phones for the squad. You should be grateful for them, not blame them for your shortcomings!"

Zengo looked down at his lap, embarrassed.

"And there better be nothing, and I mean NOTHING, amiss at tomorrow's event. And meanwhile, you've got a narwhal to find. What are you doing sitting here eating doughnuts? Every one of your tails is on the line!"

Plazinski wheeled around and left the break room, slamming the door behind him.

The Platypus Police Squad, most of them chewing the last of their snacks, looked from one to another. With that threat from Plazinski still hanging in the air, it was hard to enjoy the sweet crumbs. How would they ever get things back to normal?

Back at City Hall, with the reporters disbanded and the mayoral podium put away, Pandini beamed as he leaned back in his big fancy mayoral chair and put his feet up on his big shiny mayoral desk.

"Did you hear how upset they were about the cameras?" he asked.

"They sure didn't sound pleased, boss," said Bobby.

"Nope, they sure didn't," said Pandini as he chewed away at a piece of bamboo from the basket

on his desk. He swiveled his chair and considered the view of downtown Kalamazoo from the office window. "Tomorrow is set to go down without a hitch. Considering the sheer number of people we can expect to turn out for the event, and the trap I've set for that old traitor Benny the Tusk . . . it will be a thing of beauty. We're almost there, friends—just inches away from destroying the Platypus Police Squad, and with it our dear friend Detective Rick Zengo and the golden legacy of his grandfather Lieutenant Dailey."

"Mr. Mayor," said Irving Myers, "should we be concerned about having revealed what we know about the narwhal so soon? A nosy reporter could connect the dots all the way back to this office."

"Don't be such a Worried Wendell, Irving," crooned Pandini. "We had no choice after the PPS showed up with their warrant, and that's why we had this contingency plan. Besides, I own the media in this town. That sneaky little lizard Derek Dougherty is wrapped right around my claw. He's had it out for the Platypus Police Squad for years, and I've put enough out there to keep his eyes focused right on them. We just need to stay the course, gentlemen, and Derek Dougherty, and the public at large, will be blaming the PPS for the surveillance state of the city. They'll blame them for the fact that the narwhal hasn't been brought into custody. And they'll blame them for tomorrow's disaster as well."

SAILBOAT EXPO, 6:21 A.M.

Zengo climbed out of the squad car, tucked a polo shirt into his khaki shorts, and tied a pastel-green sweater around his neck.

"I look ridiculous," he said.

The detectives had just pulled up to the docks as the sun rose above the horizon. Pandini had put a construction crew on overnight duty to patch up the docks and get them ready for the expo. Zengo had to hand it to the tycoon-turned-politician: he sure knew how to get things done on a schedule. Food trucks and merchandise tables were already in place, ready for the tens of thousands of Kalamazooians who would be arriving. In fact, nautical buffs were already swarming the shores, setting up chairs to snag the best views of the ships that would soon be pulling into the bay.

"Nobody said undercover work was easy," said Cooper. She took a blond wig out of a duffle bag and bobby pinned it to her head. She also wore a pleated skirt and a sweater with an anchor woven into the front.

"True," Zengo said. "At least I don't look as bad as O'Malley."

"Watch yer bill, kid!" O'Malley wore a button-down shirt tucked into white pants. He placed a captain's hat atop his head. "'Tis a wonderful day to raise the sails. Cheerio! Pip-pip!"

"Hey, how long before O'Malley spills mustard on those white pants?" Zengo chuckled.

"I'd put my money on relish first," said Cooper, laughing.

O'Malley straightened his jacket. "All right, you hyenas, we're going to split up. Cooper, you take the northern piers. Zengo, you take the south side. I'll stay here, where the main road exits into the dock area."

"You mean where all the food vendors will be?" asked Zengo.

"Don't doubt my tactics, son. I need to make sure none of the food is tainted. Especially the funnel cakes." O'Malley lifted his binoculars to his eyes and scanned the water. "Looks like Diaz and Lucinni are in position."

Zengo gazed out to the horizon and spotted the

dynamic duo puttering along in a tiny motorboat. It was so small, the two of them barely fit in it.

The detectives donned their sunglasses and made their way to their posts. It wasn't long before the crowds began to swell. All was quiet across the water, barely a ripple in sight.

One thing was for sure: Pandini wasn't going to let anybody forget who was putting on this show. Banners hung on every light post, proclaiming, "Kalamazoo City's Inaugural Sailboat Expo, brought to you by Mayor Frank Pandini Jr." Still, after the press conference yesterday, it wasn't Pandini's black-and-white hide but rather the platypuses' tails that would be mounted on the wall. With a shudder, Zengo remembered Plazinski's last words from the day before.

Zengo climbed up on a pier post and tried to make himself comfortable. He tapped his earpiece to make sure that it was secure. "All clear from the south. No sign of the narwhal. Pandini's podium is set up right near me, over."

"Roger that. All clear by the access road—yes, that's right, two dogs with the works . . ."

Zengo shook his head. When O'Malley was ordering, it was never too early for the works.

Over the next hour, the crowd swelled until every pier was filled. The sun was shining, there wasn't a cloud in sight, and it was a beautiful day to be down by the water. Even Zengo was excited to see the boats.

And soon there they were, just visible on the horizon. Dozens of yachts, each more majestic than the last. The crowd roared with approval. Their cheers grew even louder when Pandini stepped up to the podium.

"Zengo, do you copy?" It was Diaz's voice in his ear. He looked out onto the water but didn't see their boat.

"Roger that, what's your twenty?" Zengo asked. A pile of seaweed hit the back of his head, followed by loud guffaws.

"Right behind you, rookie. We've been out there on the water for hours. We need to use the bathroom. Watch the cruiser for us?" He gestured to the dinky motorboat bobbing next to the dock behind them.

Zengo rolled his eyes. "Whatever. Make it quick, the show is about to start."

Lucinni saluted Zengo while Diaz tied up the boat. "Thanks, kid!" they said, and took off for the portable toilets.

Zengo turned his attention back to the bay. As the

sailboats paraded in formation toward the docks, a small ramshackle vessel weaved erratically in and around the ships. Zengo lifted his sunglasses and put his binoculars up to his eyes. It was a few teenagers in a motorboat. This was not the time to be out for a joyride. The wind was beginning to pick up, making their presence there among the huge boats even riskier. And, he noticed, not one of them was wearing a life jacket.

"Cooper, are you seeing this?" Zengo asked.

"Yup," she replied. "Diaz and Lucinni, are you on this? Bring these jokers in to shore, will ya?"

"They're not out there," said Zengo. "They're in the darn bathroom."

"What?" Cooper exclaimed.

Zengo watched tensely as the teens' boat bobbed higher and higher in the wake of the larger crafts and caught a rolling wave broadside. The boat was very near to capsizing, and if it did, the kids could get pulled under the hull of the nearby yacht. So far, the people on the docks hadn't spotted them, but they would soon. Zengo had to act quickly.

The small motorboat left behind by the chuckleheaded detectives bobbed in the choppy water behind him. Before he could think twice, he took a deep breath and stepped off the dock and into the boat, his legs shaking. "It's a standard-issue PPS watercraft," he told himself. "You're perfectly safe as long as you stay in the boat."

He yanked at the motor pull, and it coughed to life. The bow of the boat lurched forward, sending Zengo toppling head over tail into the back of the craft.

"I can do this. I can do this," said Zengo. It was almost impossible to ignore the fact that he was surrounded by water on all sides.

He glanced up at the teens. Their boat was tossed by the wake, and half of them spilled out into the waves; the other half would soon join them. The crowd finally noticed and began to shout and point. The kids were struggling to keep their heads above the surface. Zengo turned the motor to its highest throttle, hoping he would get to them in time.

The small boat sped along, and that's when Zengo saw it.

An enormous shadowy mass passed beneath his boat.

Zengo looked ahead to the struggling kids. "Help us!" they called. Zengo had to get to them quickly. He pushed the engine as hard as he could, but it was no use—the speeding shadow bolted forward and a tusk appeared above the surface. Zengo could barely look as the narwhal lowered his head at the kids and the boat beside them.

Screams came from the shore as everyone on the docks saw the tusk. The sailboats turned hard out into open water to avoid the charging narwhal, and they crashed into one another as they tried to navigate away from the docks.

The narwhal had now fully emerged from the water, revealing his face for the entire city to see. There was no mistaking: it was Benny the Tusk.

Zengo pulled out his boomerang.

"Platypus Police Squad! Freeze!"

Whether the narwhal heard or not, he kept rocketing straight toward the sinking teens. To those on the shore, it must have looked as though Benny was about to spear them. But as a huge ship passed between the docks and the drowning kids, Zengo saw the narwhal lift the teens from the sea and place them gently on some nearby rocks.

Zengo's bill hung open as the large sea beast turned to face him. Was he friend or foe? Zengo couldn't take any chances.

"Stop swimming and put your fins up!" shouted Zengo. His boomerang was locked on the narwhal's brow. He had a clear shot. That's when Benny gave out a guttural, poetic sound. The narwhal bowed his head and then slowly sank beneath the water's surface. Zengo looked around for a shadow beneath the surface, but he saw nothing. Benny was gone.

Zengo's reverie was shattered by the deafening sound of wood splintering and screams of terror coming from the docks. Zengo turned to see one of the giant yachts crash into the central pier. Out in the bay, mangled sailboats floated listlessly in the surf. Far off on the horizon, a puff of water was blown into the air.

He restarted the motor and steered his boat over to the stranded teens. As he pulled them aboard, he couldn't help but wonder: who was Benny the Tusk, really? And what was he doing here?

PLATYPUS POLICE SQUAD HEADQUARTERS, 11:31 A.M.

"ZENGO!"

The front page of the *Kalamazoo Krier* website had trouble plastered all over it. The story's headline shouted: PLATYPUS COP STANDS BY AS NARWHAL ATTACKS!

The huge color photo showed the narwhal bursting through the surface of the water, practically impaling two of the kids on his tusk. The expression on the narwhal's face was vicious. Zengo was behind the narwhal, standing in Lucinni and Diaz's boat, watching.

Zengo had been staring at that horrible photo and

headline for more than half an hour before Plazinski burst onto the squad floor to find him.

"You've got to believe me, Sarge. That is NOT how it went down!" Zengo pleaded as he and the other detectives followed the sarge into his office.

"Oh, so that's not you right there, with your bill hanging open, while some kids are practically getting killed?" barked Plazinski.

"No, that's me, but . . . the narwhal did nothing wrong! He was rescuing those kids!"

"You know what, Zengo? It doesn't matter! I don't care if the narwhal was giving them free tickets to the Sharks game—he's a fugitive and a suspect in the cruise ship disaster, and *you* let him go! And now the Platypus Police Squad's reputation is being smeared in the press! Again!" Plazinski slammed his hand down on the desk so hard that Zengo thought it might crack in half. "As far as any Kalamazooian is concerned, this is what the Platypus Police Squad is all about! We might as well be in cahoots with that fish!"

Zengo opened his bill to point out that, technically, Benny was a mammal, but he thought better of it.

O'Malley studied the photo, sighing deeply. "That's Benny all right. There's no question. But, Sarge, I think we're missing the point here. We need to be asking ourselves *why*. After all these years, why does he return now? He got away when we nabbed the rest of Pandini's gang. And not a peep from him ever since."

"Maybe he's out to collect a debt from Pandini Jr.?" Diaz suggested.

"Or maybe he and Pandini Sr. had a disagreement before he split, and now he's got some sort of revenge on his mind?" said Lucinni.

"You watch too many mobster movies," grumbled Plazinski.

"I pulled the file on Benny," said Cooper, "and there's hardly anything in it. Why wouldn't our department have more on this guy if he played such a big part in Pandini Sr.'s operation?"

"He never went to trial," said Plazinski. "If we don't—"

Whatever he was going to say next, it was cut short by his phone ringing. "It's the mayor," he said.

"Speak of the devil . . ." said Zengo.

Plazinski glared at him as he answered the phone. "Mr. Mayor. Yes . . . I'm looking at the home page right now. I know. Yes . . . the detectives are right here. . . . Yes, I know. Sure. I'll put you on speakerphone." Plazinski pressed a button on his phone and laid it on his desk. "You're on with the team."

Mayor Pandini's voice came over the phone speaker. "Greetings, Detectives."

Zengo, O'Malley, and Cooper shared an apprehensive look.

"You know how forgiving I can be with those I trust," Pandini continued. "You've all been on the receiving end of my generosity more than once. And you've earned it. But the last few weeks, and this latest display . . ." Pandini paused. "I'm calling to tell you how disappointed I am today. Your dreadful police work, and your utter failure to resolve this narwhal situation, has ruined something much bigger than some boat show—today's event was designed to lift the spirits of all our citizens and to boost our fair city's economy. I've tried to be patient with all of you; I've supported you as the media demanded your heads, but no more. I am hereby putting the entire Platypus Police Squad on notice. You have twenty-four hours to bring that narwhal to justice. One more slipup, and I'm going to have to take . . . drastic measures. Have I made myself clear?"

All five detectives reluctantly mumbled yes. But Zengo was boiling inside.

"Thank you, Detectives. This is your last chance. Don't disappoint me again." Pandini hung up with a bang so loud they all jumped.

Plazinski glared at his detectives, but Zengo couldn't hold back. "This isn't fair, Sarge. I know how it looks, but I've been thinking, and the only thing we can actually pin on the narwhal is that he tore up the dock."

"Yeah—trying to attack O'Malley's daughter!" said Plazinski.

"I know, I thought so too," said Zengo. "But did you ever think that maybe he was trying to get our attention? I mean, what's the motive here? He pops up at the most visible spot on Kalamazoo's coast, gets caught on camera, but doesn't hurt anyone. I think there's more going on here than we're seeing."

Plazinski pounded his fist on the desk again so hard the phone jumped, and the detectives did as well. "Zengo, I've heard enough baloney from you to last me a lifetime. You heard the mayor. You have exactly twenty-four hours to arrest that criminal!"

"But you're not listening," said Zengo. "Today at the boat show—the narwhal didn't attack those kids, he saved them! I was right there; I watched him! He

99

didn't act or sound anything like the monster caught on the security footage!"

"Exactly what are you suggesting?" growled Plazinski, his bill just inches from Zengo's, his eyes flaring with rage.

"We didn't get any video from the surveillance camera. What if the tape that we were given had been manipulated in some way?" Zengo looked to O'Malley for support, but Corey was just staring at him, waiting. "Neither the PPS nor the narwhal has done anything wrong, but we're both in the cross-hairs now. I'm beginning to suspect that this whole thing is a setup."

"There you go again, throwing wild accusations around," said Plazinski. "So who's behind this time, rookie? Pandini again?"

The sarge had called him "rookie," like it was still his first case. Zengo clenched his fists but couldn't come up with anything to say. Plazinski didn't believe him, as usual, and that was all there was to it.

"I got sick of your crazy ideas long ago, back when Mr. Pandini was *only* the most successful business-man in Kalamazoo. But it's different now—it's worse. Now you're talking about the mayor of our city. He

100

deserves nothing less than our trust, our respect, and our loyal service!"

Plazinski turned to the other detectives. "Now, you heard the mayor. You have twenty-four hours. Get back down to the docks—the crowd should be gone by now, and you can try picking up the narwhal's trail from there. Dismissed!"

Everyone shuffled back to their desks as quickly as they could, but Zengo remained, his eyes still locked on the big boss.

O'Malley turned and put his hand on Zengo's arm. "Hey, kid," he whispered. "Let's go. Even if you're right—and for the record, I think you might be— there's only one way we're going to prove it, and that's finding that narwhal."

Zengo looked at his partner, grateful. At least *somebody* had his back. "Okay."

O'Malley led Zengo and the other detectives out of Sergeant Plazinski's office, closing the door behind them.

The sergeant fell back in his chair and rubbed his face. He swiveled around and looked at the awards and framed photographs displayed on the wall behind his desk. Among all the others was a photo of himself with Zengo's grandfather Lieutenant Dailey.

"I'm sorry, boss," Plazinski said to the framed picture. He picked up his phone and tapped away at the buttons. "Yes, this is Sergeant Plazinski. May I speak to Mayor Pandini?"

"Hello again, Sergeant," said Pandini once he'd gotten on the line.

"Mr. Mayor—" Plazinski started.

"How many times do I have to tell you to call me Frank? Now, are they in position?"

"Yes, you really lit a fire under their tails. They should be down by the docks within the hour."

"Good, good," said Pandini. "You've done well, Sergeant. Just a little longer now, and we'll both have exactly what we've always wanted."

KALAMAZOO CITY DOCKS, 12:10 P.M.

"So you really believe me?" asked Zengo from the passenger seat. "You think the narwhal is being set up?"

"I think that this story is more complicated than the sarge and the mayor think it is," O'Malley said. "The narwhal has had plenty of opportunities to hurt people, and he hasn't. That said, I'm not sure I believe that Benny the Tusk is some sort of saint now. You weren't here years back when that narwhal terrorized Kalamazoo. If he hadn't disappeared when he did, this city might still be under Pandini Sr.'s thumb. And what about the cruise ship? If Benny didn't make that hole in the hull, then what did?"

"I get it, believe me. I don't know all the answers, I don't know what Benny is up to, but I know what I saw. He saved those teenagers from drowning. I looked him directly in the eyes, and I'm telling you, he wanted to tell me something."

O'Malley parked the squad car in an alleyway adjacent to the harbor. "Well, I'm not sure I completely believe it, but like I said, there's only one way to find out." He threw open the driver's side door. "Let's go. Cooper, Diaz, and Lucinni will be here soon, and we don't want them finding all the best evidence, do we?"

The detectives stepped out of the car and walked down to the pier. They soon noticed that all the dockworkers were glaring at them angrily.

"Hey, it's the Platypus Police Squad, right on time," said a fisherman, hauling equipment onto a small ship. "The boat show attack was only *four hours ago*."

"We're working on it, sir," said O'Malley.

Another fisherman stepped in front of the detectives. "You realize that narwhal's scaring away all the fish? And thanks to him, nobody wants to ship their goods through Kalamazoo City right now either. He's putting all of us out of work. And what do you do? You stand there while he gets away."

"With all due respect, sir, there's information here you're not privy to—"

The fisherman called out to a couple of his fellow crew members. "Hey! Linda, AJ! You hearin' this malarkey the cops are tryin' to feed me?"

"It stinks worse than this port at sunset," said one of them as she pulled a bucket of bait fish over the side of the boat. The rest of her friends laughed.

Zengo didn't have anything to say in response. As much as he wanted to explain himself to them, maybe they were right. The narwhal was a fugitive, innocent or not, and he'd failed to catch him.

The fishermen all got on their boat and set out to sea. O'Malley started to make his way toward the last pier, closest to where the narwhal breached the surface earlier that day. Zengo was about to join him, but that's when he noticed something in the water, behind the boat.

"O'Malley! Look!" Zengo took two steps and grabbed his partner, pointing about fifty yards past the end of the nearest dock. As the retreating fishing vessel moved toward open water, a tusk slowly rose from the waters behind it.

"That's got to be him," said O'Malley. Sweat beaded up on his brow, and he drew his boomerang from his holster. Zengo pulled his out as well—just in case—and waited for the narwhal's head to breach the surface.

Before it did, though, there was a *BANG*. The ship lurched as the narwhal slammed against it from under the water.

"He's trying to sink them!" shouted O'Malley, raising his weapon.

There was another loud noise, and the ship thrust again toward the starboard side. The fishermen

gripped the sides of the ship as it threatened to capsize and spill them all overboard.

There was one more crash, and the ship tilted sideways as its engine died. It came to a stop a few dozen yards off its course.

"They're sitting ducks now!" said O'Malley. "Rick, we've got to get that thing's attention, or it's going to kill everyone on board!"

The tusk emerged once more from the water, but it didn't head in the direction of the boat. Instead, it turned and headed in the opposite direction—right at Zengo and O'Malley.

"We better scram, kid!" cried O'Malley.

"Roger that, old-timer!"

The detectives leaped out of the way and tumble-rolled into the gravel parking lot. They turned to see if the narwhal would smash the dock again, but just as the tusk came into the shallow water, it stopped and sank below the waves. The water became still once more.

"What the heck was that?" asked O'Malley from behind a barrel.

"I . . . I don't know," said Zengo as he rushed to his feet. He squinted out at the water. The fishermen were waving to him from their halted boat, shouting for him to come rescue them.

"Okay, okay!" he shouted. But just as he made a move toward the harbormaster's office, there was yet another loud, wrenching noise. Up from the water, just to the left of where the fishing boat had come to a stop, rose a huge chunk of twisted metal. Zengo and O'Malley watched with their bills dropped as the giant piece of debris raised up out of the bay. The narwhal's head was just below, straining to keep the metal above the surface.

"What's he doing?" O'Malley said.

"I think that's . . . a piece of the cruise ship," said

Zengo. "You can see the markings on the metal. The cleaning crews must have missed it."

"It was just under the surface, right where the ship had been heading." O'Malley's eyes went wide. "If the fishing boat had hit it, it would have ripped its hull to shreds."

Zengo and his partner shared a look. "Do you believe me now?" Zengo said.

They both turned back to the water as Benny the Tusk raised a fin out of the water, then sank back below the surface and disappeared.

MULLIGAN'S, 7:22 P.M.

By the time O'Malley and Zengo had called in Cooper, Diaz, and Lucinni, rescued the fishermen, and supervised the removal of the cruise ship debris from the bay, they were completely bushed. But they knew they couldn't call it a day—not with the narwhal still out there. So they went to refuel at their favorite greasy spoon—Mulligan's. They knew they didn't have long to meet Pandini's demands, but after what had happened that afternoon, it was clear this wouldn't be as simple as slapping cuffs on Benny (which didn't seem all that simple anyway).

Brenda, usually so happy to see them, barely looked them in the eyes as she took their order. Zengo was crushed. He knew the entire city was starting to turn on them—but he never imagined Brenda, of all people, would give them the cold shoulder.

On the tabletop, Zengo's phone, which never left his sight, began to vibrate, twirling in a circle. It was Cooper. He picked it up on the third rotation.

"What do you have?" he said.

"I've got an update on the search for the narwhal," she said. "Where are you?"

"We're at Mulligan's."

"That figures," she said. "Make sure nobody can hear what I'm about to tell you."

Zengo looked around. Nobody sat near them. O'Malley's food had just arrived, and he was tucking a napkin into the neck of his shirt.

"Yup, no chance anyone else is paying attention. What's up?"

"I was upset with myself for arriving too late to be there with you when the narwhal arrived, and so I paid a visit to our favorite hot dog stand to see if I could once again borrow some footage and see what happened for myself."

114

"Did Andy give you the footage from this afternoon?"

"I think he would have—if there had been any footage to give. When he tried to access the files, they didn't exist."

That didn't make any sense. "Pandini's security system is state of the art. There's no way it just turned off or glitched out."

"I agree. That's when I politely asked Andy to step aside and took a look at the system files myself. A few minutes before I'd gotten there, someone had accessed the dock security footage for the afternoon, downloaded it, and deleted the originals!"

Zengo was speechless. Was someone in Pandini's inner circle connected to Benny somehow? He couldn't figure out how the pieces all fit together.

"Get down to the station," Cooper continued. "We'll work this up. Maybe it'll lead us to the narwhal before tomorrow's deadline!"

"On it!" Zengo disconnected the call, reached into his pocket, and threw a couple of bills on the table. "Let's vamoose!" he said to his partner as he scooted out of the diner bench.

O'Malley wiped his mouth and slid out too. "What's up?"

115

Zengo spoke in a low voice. "I'll tell you in the car. We need to get back to headquarters."

The detectives hustled out of Mulligan's, striding past the handful of patrons sitting at the counter. Zengo's eye caught a familiar sight on the flat-screen televisions—the Platypus Police Squad shield. He

stopped dead in his tracks, and O'Malley bumped into him. They both gaped at the headline written across the bottom of the screen: PLATYPUS COPS: KALAMAZOO CITY IS A "DUMP."

"Quiet down, everybody!" Brenda turned up the volume. She threw a dirty glare at Zengo and O'Malley.

The grim face of reporter Max Pearson appeared on the screen. "In this exclusive surveillance video footage obtained by Action News, the detectives who have been shirking their responsibilities in bringing the narwhal to justice insult the city that they are sworn to protect."

The surveillance footage from that afternoon at the docks began to roll. Though the camera was capturing them from the rear, Zengo recognized himself and his partner, talking to the dockworkers just a few hours earlier.

"You are the scum we're supposed to protect?" said O'Malley.

"Man, I hate this city. What a dump," said Zengo.

Zengo and O'Malley looked at each other in astonishment. That was them on the screen, but there was no way those were their words. Except the voices were unmistakably their own. Someone must have doctored the footage—the same person who had downloaded it before Cooper could access it.

The camera now switched to a live feed of Max Pearson reporting from the docks. "It was here that the Platypus Police Squad, charged with saving our fair city from a dangerous menace, instead spent their time berating innocent, hardworking Kalamazoo City citizens. Then, immediately afterward, it got even worse."

The fishing boat was now shown sailing out toward open water. The two detectives' backs were once again facing the camera.

"Narwhal, come in, narwhal," said a voice that sounded like Zengo's. "Destroy the boat!"

Then just as it actually happened, the narwhal's tusk emerged from the water, and the boat was rocked as the narwhal slammed into it. That's when the footage cut out.

The crowd at Mulligan's gasped as the news report came to a close. They grew enraged—and rowdy. A hamburger, loaded with the works, splatted on the back of O'Malley's head.

"Kid, let's get out of here!" he said, shoving Zengo ahead of him as he wiped the mess off the back of his head. The detectives shot out of Mulligan's as fast as their webbed feet could carry them, dodging heaps of mashed potatoes and bowls of chowder all the way. They jumped in their squad car, O'Malley revved the engine, and they peeled out of the driveway.

As they drove to PPS headquarters, Zengo filled O'Malley in on his phone call with Cooper.

"This is getting fishier by the minute," said O'Malley.

"Someone is clearly out to get us," said Zengo. "Someone with access to Pandini's security footage. But who?"

By the time they reached Platypus Police Squad headquarters, every media outlet in town was camped outside.

"Ah, crud," said O'Malley as he parked the car. "Too bad we don't have a giant flyswatter to get rid of these pests. Let's go. And not a word to anybody! Keep your bill low!"

The journalists swarmed to capture Zengo and O'Malley on film. They all shouted questions at once.

"Do you have a comment on the surveillance footage?"

"Why do you hate Kalamazoo City so much?"

"Why are you conspiring with the narwhal?"

O'Malley and Zengo shoved through the crowd and reached the entrance. They were just about to disappear inside when Derek Dougherty stepped forward and asked, "Detective Rick Zengo, what is your comment on your grandfather's portrait being removed from the wall in PPS headquarters? Is it true that Lieutenant Dailey conspired against our fair city?"

Zengo was gobsmacked. His *grandfather* was being brought into this? Derek pushed his microphone in his bill, but Zengo threw it to the ground and slammed the front door shut behind him.

Once inside Platypus Police Squad headquarters, he saw it was true—Peggy was in the midst of taking down the memorial to his heroic grandfather. "What on earth is happening?" demanded Zengo.

Peggy looked down at her shoes, speechless. A single tear ran down her cheek.

Zengo and O'Malley headed to the bullpen to find Cooper, Diaz, and Lucinni. But none of them were there. In fact, there wasn't one other platypus in the entire station.

That's when Frank Pandini Jr. emerged from the sergeant's office.

"Zengo, O'Malley, I have some unfortunate news. Your services are no longer required by Kalamazoo City."

"What?" exclaimed the two detectives in unison.

"The Platypus Police Squad has officially been dismantled," said Pandini.

"But who will protect the city?" asked Zengo.

The door from the briefing room swung open. Out marched an army of penguins in uniform. Zengo glanced at their shiny new badges.

"*Penguin Police Force*?" he said aloud.

"This city needs a team that can protect us from

crime, no matter where it rears its head: land or water. For decades, we have relied on the platypuses to do this." He shook his head. "But it's clear to me—and to all the citizens of Kalamazoo City—we can no longer trust the platypuses. And with so much trouble coming in from our waters, and more urgency than ever to resolve it, it is time to bring in a team that's not afraid to get their flippers wet."

A large black-suited penguin with a bright-orange beak stepped forward. He whipped off his aviator sunglasses. His steely gaze pierced the newly disgraced detectives. "Greetings. I am Sergeant Brayden Baghai with the Penguin Police Force." Sergeant Baghai held out his flipper. "Your badges and boomerangs, please."

ZENGO HOUSE, 8:59 A.M.

Even though Rick Zengo had his own apartment,
sometimes he just needed to crash at his parents'
house. He nursed the hot chocolate his mom had put
in front of him, sipping from his favorite childhood
mug—the clown mug he had won at the Kalamazoo
City carnival when he was a kid.

"Aww, Ricky. This will all sort itself out," said his
mother. "Well . . . somehow. I hope."

"Thanks, Mom," he said as he added another handful of marshmallows to his mug.

"Chin up, Ricky. Maybe you want to go for a run?"

asked Zengo's dad as he wiped sweat from his brow. He had just gotten back from his morning jog, but he was happy to head out again.

Zengo nodded to the television, which was running nonstop coverage of the disgraced detectives and the newly appointed Penguin Police Force. "I'm probably better off keeping a low profile."

Zengo's mother turned it off.

"I just don't believe those reports," said Zengo's mother. "You love this city, Ricky! Why would you ever say such things about it?"

"Exactly! I never would!"

"But Ricky . . ." said his father cautiously, looking for the right words, ". . . how would they have gotten such a thing on tape then?"

"I don't know. But I guess it doesn't matter now." He put his spoon down and wiped his bill. "Thanks for breakfast, guys. Is it okay if I grab some of my old things from the attic?"

"Of course, Ricky. Help yourself," said his mother.

Zengo left his parents' kitchen and dragged his feet up the stairs to the second floor. In the hallway outside his old bedroom, he pulled on the chain that dangled from the ceiling. A ladder folded down, and

Zengo climbed up. He ducked his head to avoid hitting it on the beams as he flicked on a light switch.

All around him was a museum of his family's history. There was his first bicycle, bins of old Halloween costumes, a box full of pictures he'd drawn when he was in kindergarten. Zengo wanted to grab some mementos from his days at the police academy. With all this clutter, it would be like finding a needle in a haystack. But it wasn't like Zengo had a job anymore. He had the time.

He sifted through a box filled with his grade school report cards and another filled with clippings of his high school accomplishments. Then he found a box filled with old greeting cards. He smiled at the sight of his grandfather's handwriting on a card that read "Happy birthday to my #1 grandson!" Actually, Zengo was his grandfather's only grandson, but that didn't matter. The sight of his grandfather's handwriting filled Zengo with warmth and despair, in equal measure. *I'm sorry I failed you, Grandpa*, he thought.

Zengo wished that there were some way that he could speak to his grandfather. Ask him what he loved about his job, and also what scared him. Find out what it was like to take down Pandini Sr. But at the

same time, he was glad his grandfather wasn't alive to see a Pandini in the mayor's office.

At the bottom of a stack of shoe boxes was one with his grandfather's handwriting scrawled across the side. It read, "Paperwork." Zengo carefully slid that box out of the stack. He blew dust off the box, thrilled to reclaim a little bit of his grandfather's history that would have been lost to time.

The familiar smell of his grandfather's aftershave

lotion hit him the moment he opened the box. Inside were stacks of letters. But they didn't have his grandfather's handwriting. Zengo picked one up and began to read.

Dear Lieutenant Dailey,

This will be my final piece of correspondence with you before I depart. I hope that the information I've provided proves to be beneficial in your case against Frank Pandini. I have come to understand that he is cruel and ruthless and deserves to spend his days behind bars.

He will be receiving a shipment of stolen goods tonight, shortly after midnight. He will expect me to be there, keeping watch. But I will be well on my way to a new life in a distant land.

I will keep an eye on you and this fair city from time to time. Had you not intervened, I don't know how I would have escaped Pandini's clutches. I owe you a great debt.

Sincerely,

Benny

Zengo read the letter again and again. Then he looked at the other contents of the box. It was filled with letters and paperwork regarding Benny the Tusk—not a criminal, like everyone had thought, but an informant, working with the Platypus Police Squad to bring down Frank Pandini Sr. And because Lieutenant Dailey was killed in that midnight raid on Pandini's shipment, no one ever knew. Benny wasn't out to hurt anyone then, and Zengo was more certain than ever that he wasn't out to hurt anyone now.

But why had he come back?

"It's up to me," Zengo said aloud. He needed to get this info to O'Malley—and fast. He pulled out his smartphone and opened his contacts list. But as soon as he found O'Malley's number, he paused.

Someone had been able to get a sample of his voice and insert it into that video. What if it sounded so much like Zengo because it *was* Zengo? Could someone be recording his phone calls?

Zengo looked around him, and his eyes wandered out the attic window. A parked car sat across the street, directly opposite the Zengos' house. How had he not noticed it before? He reached for an old pair of binoculars for a closer look.

130

Somebody was in the driver's seat, sitting motion-less, his eyes hidden under a hat. Someone with a black suit and an orange penguin beak.

ZENGOS' DRIVEWAY, 10:18 A.M.

Zengo's father backed his SUV out of the garage. He pulled onto the road, slowly passing the car that had been parked across the street since sunrise. Back in the top floor of the house, Rick Zengo was silhouetted against the old drapery, his head facing down at the street. Mr. Zengo turned the car onto Franklin Avenue and headed downtown.

A muffled voice came from under a heap of blankets in the backseat. "Are they following you?"

Zengo's dad looked in the rearview mirror. "I don't see anybody."

Detective Zengo pushed the blankets aside. "Good. But I don't know how long we've got before they realize that shape in the attic window is just some clothes draped over cardboard boxes. Turn left up here to get to the docks."

"Are you sure about this, Rick?"

"Yes, Dad. O'Malley isn't answering his phone. And I imagine that he's being monitored, as well as the rest of the former PPS. I don't want to risk going over to his house until I have some actual concrete evidence. And that means tracking down Benny the Tusk on my own."

"But don't you think the Penguin Police Force will be patrolling the docks?"

"Probably. But the docks are pretty busy this time of day, and I brought a disguise. My plan is to slip onto a boat, get out into the harbor, and find that narwhal."

"But how can you be sure he's not going to try to attack you again?"

"He's had plenty of chances to hurt people and he hasn't. There has to be a reason why he is back now. And whatever he did in the past, one thing's for sure—Grandpa trusted him. At least at the end of his life. If I'm going to get to the bottom of this, I think I've got to start trusting him too."

Mr. Zengo approached an intersection. The light turned red. "Get down, son," he warned.

Zengo quickly grabbed the blankets and covered himself once more. He took a deep breath and remained still, his eyes locked on the thin strip of light he left from under his camouflage.

The SUV came to a stop beside a police cruiser. Mr. Zengo nodded politely to the officer behind the wheel. The penguin just glared back suspiciously. Zengo's dad kept his hands on the wheel and looked forward. When the light turned green, he gently stepped on the gas pedal. The cruiser took a left while Zengo and his dad continued straight.

"That was a close one." Zengo's dad glanced back in the rearview mirror at the heap of blankets. "You sure you can pull this off?"

Zengo poked his head out from the blankets again.

"I have to, Dad. I'm the only one who can."

"But, Ricky . . . you're not a detective anymore. You're operating outside of the system."

"I'll never not be a detective, Dad. And the system— it's broken right now. Somebody in the mayor's office, maybe even the mayor himself, is lying to the people of Kalamazoo City. I aim to find out why."

Zengo's father dropped him off a few blocks away from the harbor. Before stepping out of the car, the former detective tucked his tail into his pants and pulled a wool cap down closely over his brow. Using some leftover Halloween face paint, he turned his bill bright yellow. He nodded good-bye to his father and let himself out of the car.

Zengo quacked to himself as he walked toward the water, limping on his left foot as he went. He figured if he appeared to be nothing more threatening than an elderly duck who muttered under his breath, nobody would come near him.

At the harbor, Zengo approached a boat rental counter. He slapped a twenty-dollar bill on the counter.

"I'd like to rent a rowboat, please," he said.

"Sure," said the guy working the booth. "I'll just

need you to fill out this form. And I'll need to see a driver's license."

"What's that now?" Zengo hadn't expected this.

"Yeah, new rules direct from the Penguin Police Force. City Hall wants to keep track of everybody who is looking to get out on the water. Narwhal attacks

and all." He pushed a clipboard toward Zengo. "Fill this out, and let me take a quick look at your license."

Uh-oh.

Zengo patted his pockets. "Darn, you know what, kiddo? I think I must've left mine at home. Wasn't expecting to need it today."

The booth operator pulled the clipboard back. "Sorry, sir. No license, no boat."

Zengo gave the kid a long look and slowly turned away from the booth. The harbor swarmed with uniformed penguins. There was no way Zengo would get away with renting a rowboat under his own identity. If he handed that guy his driver's license, he would not only reveal that he wasn't a duck, but he would also probably pop up on some sort of watch list. And with all the surveillance on the dock, he would never be able to sneak onto a boat without a rental. But Zengo was determined to get out on that water. He finally decided to employ a time-honored persuasion technique.

Bribery.

He stepped back up to the ticket counter and plopped down another twenty-dollar bill.

"Does this count as ID, son?"

"I'm sorry, sir, I can't—"

Zengo put down two more twenties and cocked an eyebrow. The guy working the booth scratched his head, looked around nervously, and slipped the clipboard back to Zengo. "Congratulations, sir. You've just rented yourself a boat." He handed Zengo a pair of oars and a day rental sticker.

Now all Zengo had to do was make his way offshore without drawing attention to himself. He took a deep breath, stepped into the craft, and soon was maneuvering the tippy little rowboat out into the harbor. Sweat dripped from his brow, but he didn't dare take off his wool cap. He could not risk detection by either the prying eyes of the Penguin Police Force or by Pandini's security cameras. He was just another duck rowing a boat into the horizon. Nothing to see here.

As he moved from the harbor area out into deeper waters, he nodded pleasantly to the fishing captains

pulling in their hauls. He dipped his head at pleasure boaters, some of whom responded with friendly honks of their air horns.

Luckily, the waters were calm. Zengo soon found himself far offshore with the KC skyline shrinking on the horizon. There wasn't another ship to be seen. *This had better work*, he thought. Otherwise he'd come out all this way for nothing.

He looked over the boat's edge and pulled out an empty paper towel tube, holding it up to his mouth like a megaphone.

"Benny? Are you out here? I'm . . . a friend."

The water remained still.

"My name is Rick Zengo. I'm Lieutenant Dailey's grandson. It's okay, I'm on your side. I want to help you."

Nothing.

Zengo sat back in the boat to wait, and he realized for the first time that he had been in such a hurry to get out on the water, he hadn't thought to rent a life jacket. Sitting on the calm bay, it was easy to put his fear of water out of his mind.

No, that couldn't last. The wind picked up, waves began to swell, and his little craft started to rock and roll. He grabbed the edge of the boat and let out a high-pitched shriek, hoping no one could hear him.

Then there was a monstrous splash, and Zengo turned quickly, nearly falling out of the boat.

In an instant, he was eye to eye with Kalamazoo City's Most Wanted Creature.

"You're Lieutenant Dailey's grandson," said Benny, his voice a low rumble. "I'd know that bill anywhere."

Up close, the creature was absolutely enormous. But Zengo felt a rush of good feeling toward this magnificent marine mammal who shared his love for his late grandfather.

"I found my grandpa's file on you," said Zengo. "He wouldn't have been able to bring Pandini to justice without you. But you disappeared. . . . Why did you come back?"

"Because if Frank Pandini Jr. succeeds, he'll fulfill the plans his father set into motion so many years ago. Complete control of Kalamazoo City."

"What is he doing?"

"He already came to control Kalamazoo's economy through a mix of legal and illegal practices. The illegal fish trade ring that you took down in your first case? He was behind that. Now that he's taken control of the political system . . . there's no limit to his power."

"But what stake do you have in any of this?" Zengo asked.

"I got in deep with Pandini's father. I helped him with his illegal shipping activities in the waters, and he paid me well. But your grandfather . . . he convinced me to go clean. To see all the harm Pandini was doing. And he gave me a fresh start, far, far away. I watched Pandini's son rise to power in Kalamazoo, and I did nothing. It didn't seem like it was my place.

But when word got to me that he had become the head of government here . . . that's when I knew he was after more than just money. He wants revenge."

"What does Pandini Jr. know about you?" asked Zengo.

"He knows I sold out his father," said Benny. "But he doesn't know that I have tracked his every move—for years."

"How?"

"I left Kalamazoo City, but everything travels by

water. I've been able to watch every boat that has come in and out of this harbor. Out here, in the open water, you can become invisible, as long as you keep your tusk down. So I lurked just below the surface and listened to everything."

Benny threw a zipped plastic sandwich bag into Zengo's boat. Zengo picked it up. Inside was a piece of plastic with two holes in it.

"What's this?"

"Pandini isn't the only one who's been recording people's conversations," said Benny. "That contains proof of every underhanded, illegal act Frank Pandini Jr. has perpetrated for years. You'll find all the evidence you need on that to bring him to justice."

"No, I mean . . . what is this thing?"

"Oh." Benny smirked. "It's a cassette tape. I record everything on them. Those new digital gizmos . . . never trusted them."

Zengo flipped the tape around in his webbed hand. He didn't even know how he'd listen to this ancient thing. Why is everyone he knows such a dinosaur when it comes to technology?

That's when he realized—O'Malley! His partner still listened to his collection of classic rock tapes in

his old car! Zengo tucked the cassette into his jacket
pocket.

"Thank you," he said.

Benny smiled, but then his face dropped. He was
looking at something over Zengo's shoulder.

A periscope had popped up directly behind Zengo.
Before he could even register what he was looking at,
the periscope became a full-fledged submarine. The
central escape hatch opened, and Sergeant Brayden
Baghai popped out.

"Thank you for leading us right to
the narwhal." He adjusted his
sunglasses. "Too bad you just
lost your job—I think you've
got a real knack for detective
work."

"Can it, Brayden," Zengo shot back. "You have to listen to me: Benny isn't what he seems—"

"Save it for the judge, Zengo. You're both under arrest."

Just then, another hatch on the submarine popped open and Derek Dougherty emerged, already snapping photos. "Nice getup, Ricky. What are you supposed to be, a puffin? More important: are you still going to deny any involvement with the narwhal?"

More submarines were surfacing, penguins scrambling out of every hatch. Zengo was frozen with nowhere to go. A penguin with a large propulsion gun shot a net at Benny, which quickly enveloped his body. The narwhal struggled to escape, but the more he wiggled, the tighter the net got.

"Run!" he shouted to Zengo.

"Run?" cried Zengo. "Where?" He looked at the deep, dark water. He had no other choice.

He took a deep breath and leaped.

The moment he hit the water, his disguise disappeared. The cap fell off, the face paint washed away, and Zengo's tail unfurled and spread out behind him. He cut through the water like a steel blade as his natural instincts took over. He didn't have time to look behind him to see if the penguins were in pursuit. He just swam—as fast as his webbed feet would propel him.

O'MALLEY HOUSE, 12:02 P.M.

Zengo pounded on O'Malley's door, a pool of water forming around his feet from his drenched clothing. There was no response. He checked the street; O'Malley's old clunker of a car was parked in front of the house. He was definitely home. Zengo looked in the window. There was his former partner, asleep on the couch, surrounded by a litter of wrappers from Frank's Franks. Zengo sighed. That was how Corey O'Malley had spent his time since their badges were confiscated and they were kicked off the force.

Zengo knocked again. He heard Karen O'Malley's voice. "Coming . . ."

She opened the door a crack to see who it was. Zengo quickly slipped past her. "Sorry, I'm in a rush!" Now Zengo was dripping water all over the O'Malleys' foyer. He looked down. "Sorry!" he said again. He sped toward the living room.

"I'll get you a towel," said Karen, picking a piece of seaweed from the carpet.

Zengo stepped over the kids' backpacks that were lying in the hallway and shook his partner by the shoulder. O'Malley opened his bleary eyes. He smelled like he could use a shower. But maybe that was just old onions on the hot dog wrappers.

He sat up and looked at Zengo in surprise. "Yeesh! You take a long walk off a short pier?"

"Sort of," Zengo replied. He pulled the cassette tape out of his back pocket. "Do you have anything that I can play this on, or should I head to the Kalamazoo City Museum?"

"A cassette! Did you hit up a yard sale?"

"No, this is from Benny."

"Are you serious?"

Zengo nodded. "I think this may be the evidence we've been looking for—the key to what's been happening in this city since Pandini became mayor."

O'Malley sprang up, spilling hot dog wrappers across the floor. "Let me see that!" He swiped the cassette from Zengo and walked across the room. He opened a closet door, and an avalanche of old wires and gizmos spilled out. "Rule number one: never throw anything away. You never know when you'll need it." Behind a stack of Atari games was an ancient boom box. "I knew this was in here somewhere," he said. He popped open the cassette door. "Aww, look,

honey," he said, pulling out a dusty cassette. "Here's that mixtape I made you back in high school." He held it out to Karen with a sentimental grin.

Zengo nabbed the mixtape and placed it in his back pocket. He didn't have time for a trip down memory lane right now. He thrust the other cassette into O'Malley's hand. "Great, great," he said. "But right now we gotta listen to this. It's important!"

O'Malley threw in the tape from Zengo and pressed Play.

Crackles and hisses came from the speakers.

Zengo strained to listen. He could make out the sound of crashing waves and a distant foghorn. Then two voices, neither familiar.

"We'll be docking in a few minutes. Are the goods hidden?"

"Twenty crates of illegal fish heading to Bamboo."

"Good. Pandini will be pleased. Delicious fish and delicious profits."

Zengo's eyes widened. He leaned forward. "Bamboo? Does that mean Pandini was involved in the illegal fish trade after all? Could he be the one behind everything happening in KC right now?"

"I don't know, Rick," said O'Malley, "but it looks like there's a lot more where this came from on this tape. I'm betting we'll find out."

Just then, a knock sounded at the front door. O'Malley was quick to click the Stop button on his deck.

The knock came again, louder and more insistent. A voice called. "Penguin Police Force! Open the door!"

Karen was already crossing the room. She looked back at O'Malley. "What should we do?" she asked.

"Open it," he said, nodding to the front door. "But stall."

"Okay." She brushed her hair back, took a deep breath, and opened the door a crack.

Zengo and O'Malley crept to the window. There were three penguins in uniform—and they looked as menacing as it is possible for penguins to look.

"May I help you?" Karen asked.

"We have a warrant for the arrest of Rick Zengo," said the lead penguin.

"And we have reason to believe he is on your property," said another, brandishing a document emblazoned with the new Penguin Police Force badge. "We have a search warrant too."

"I-I-I'm sorry, but . . . I haven't seen anyone come in the house today." Karen's eyes drifted to the side.

The lead penguin seized that moment to shove the door open and brush Karen aside. They quickly scurried into the living room.

There was nobody there.

Baby Lissy began to cry, and Declan and Jonathan ran out of their rooms. They glanced at their mother, and the look on her face told them to keep their bills shut. Karen followed the penguin officers from room to room.

"I told you," she said, "Rick Zengo is not here. We haven't seen him in days."

"And what about your husband? Where is he?"

Karen just shook her head. "I . . . don't know."

"You know obstruction of justice is a crime, ma'am. If we find your husband or his old partner on these premises . . ."

Karen looked around for a moment, then burst into tears. "Corey hasn't been himself lately." She took a moment, and then threw in some more sobs. "He hasn't been home in days."

Declan and Jonathan caught on to their mom's plan, hugging her. Jonathan looked at the officers. "It's been really hard on her."

"Dad is . . . depressed," said Declan, gesturing at

the Frank's Franks wrappers spewed across the floor.

"I'm very sorry," said one of the officers, in a gentle voice.

"My dad ate hot dogs when he was depressed too," said the tall officer.

"Ma'am, if your husband does turn up, and if there is any news about Rick Zengo, we beg you to contact us right away, for your husband's own good, and for the good of his former partner as well."

"I will," said Karen, sobbing even harder now. The officers let themselves out of the house and closed the door behind them. They jumped into their cruiser and gunned the engine, oblivious to the fact that the beat-up old car that had been parked in front of the house was now missing.

KALAMAZOO CITY STREETS, 12:44 P.M.

"Slow down, old-timer," said Zengo. "Keep it below the speed limit. Rule number one: we're not cops anymore. We can't be drawing attention to ourselves."

"You're right," sighed O'Malley. "Man, I just want to throw on the ol' siren and cruise!"

Zengo and O'Malley both wore baseball hats tipped low on their brows as they maneuvered through the city streets. Zengo slouched down as much as he could, O'Malley's boom box perched on his stomach, and scanned their surroundings for any signs of the penguins in black.

159

"Try Cooper again," said O'Malley. "We're approaching her neighborhood."

"Okay." Zengo took out his personal cell phone and scrolled down his contacts list to find Jo Cooper's entry. He clicked on the phone icon.

On the other end of the line, Cooper's cell phone rang on her kitchen counter. All the lights in her apartment were off, all her windows were closed with the shades drawn, except for one, which was open and let in a light breeze.

Her phone continued to ring. A flipper reached forward and picked it up—a flipper that belonged to Sergeant Brayden Baghai of the Penguin Police Force.

A smile spread across his beak at the sight of Rick Zengo's name on the screen. Behind Sergeant Baghai was a flurry of activity, as officers ransacked Cooper's apartment looking for clues as to where the special investigator might have disappeared to.

Sergeant Baghai answered the phone.

"Cooper!" said Zengo. "You're there!"

"Good afternoon, Mr. Zengo. I'm glad you called— we've been looking for you."

Zengo froze, the blood draining from his tail. "Is that you, Baghai?"

"Indeed. Ms. Cooper is not here at the moment, but we'll find her soon enough. In the meantime, perhaps you would like to swing by her apartment to turn yourself in?"

"Give me that phone," barked O'Malley. He swiped it and threw it out the car window. The phone crashed on the pavement and shattered under the tire of a passing car.

"My phone!" cried Zengo.

"Quit yer crying," said O'Malley. "I guarantee they were putting a trace on it. It was only going to get us caught. We need to find Cooper. And we need to ditch this car. It won't take them long to figure out we're driving it around and put an APB on it."

"Should we head to Mulligan's?" suggested Zengo. "Wait. No—they'll definitely look for us there."

"If I know Cooper, she'll be looking for us. And she won't go looking in any of the obvious places."

"What about Diaz and Lucinni's house? That would be the last place either of us would go looking for help."

"And if the Penguin Police Force are trying to arrest anyone on the PPS who has a clue, they probably won't be tracking those two knuckleheads," said O'Malley. "I never thought I'd say this, but we need them right now."

"I know exactly where they'll be," said Zengo. "Hang a left up here on Jefferson Boulevard."

O'Malley stepped on the gas to beat a yellow light and cut the wheel. There was no time to waste.

LUCKY STRIKE BOWLING ALLEY, 1:38 P.M.

Lucinni slouched in his seat while Diaz focused on the pins at the end of the lane. The two former detectives were dressed in identical lime-green-and-cream bowling-league uniforms. Their team name, the Platy-pins, was embroidered across the back. Diaz held the bowling ball steady, took a deep breath, and rolled it down the lane. The ball bumped down the middle and then took a sharp left into the gutter. It was the fifth gutter ball he had thrown that day. He was crushed.

"You're up," Diaz said despondently. Lucinni stood

165

up, nacho crumbs falling to the floor as he did.

"That roll was disgraceful!" said Zengo, stepping into their lane, carrying the boom box. O'Malley picked at the leftover nachos on the side table.

"Not our best game," agreed Diaz. "But I doubt you chumps could do better."

"We could do WAY better," said Zengo.

"Check this out!" said O'Malley, taking the cassette tape out of the boom box and flashing it at his ex-squad mates.

"What's that?" asked Lucinni. "Wait, let me guess: you two started an a cappella group, and that's your demo! What are you calling yourselves? The Monotone Monotremes?"

Zengo was kind of relieved that these two clowns still had some life in them. He grabbed the tape and put it in his pocket. "No," he whispered. "This is the key to figuring out what's happening in Kalamazoo City, and who's behind it."

"How's that?" asked Diaz as he crossed his arms.

"We'll explain later," said Zengo. "But we need to go—now. Do you have a car we can use?"

"No," said Diaz, looking at his feet. "I, uh, lost mine in a bet. Not my best game of bowling."

"And my car got repossessed," said Lucinni.

Zengo sighed. These guys. "Well, we've got to get out of here as soon as we can. The Penguin Police Force is hot on our tails. We ditched O'Malley's car around back. They're likely not far behind."

"Guess we'll have to head out on foot," said Diaz. He took the ball out of Lucinni's hand and threw it down the alley. The pins crashed against one another. "Hey! I finally rolled a strike!"

"Oh, and leave your phones behind," said Zengo.

"No way!" said Lucinni. "I've got a million games on here!"

"They're likely tracking us, Bubba," said O'Malley. He took the phone out of Lucinni's hand and threw it in the trash. "We don't have a choice."

"Ugh, fine," said Diaz, reaching into his pocket.

The four friends darted toward the door but then stopped short. Blue lights swirled in the parking lot. Sirens screamed.

"Dang! They're here already!" said Zengo. "Is there another way out of this place?"

"The emergency exit is next to the bathrooms," said Lucinni. "C'mon!"

"This is an emergency if I've ever seen one," said Zengo as they raced across the lobby of the bowling alley. When they reached the bright-red door, Zengo took a deep breath and pushed on the handle.

He took a right, but his way was blocked by a shadowy figure. Zengo turned to run to the left, but was grabbed by his collar and pulled out into the parking lot.

"Where do you think you're going?" said a familiar voice. Zengo looked behind him.

It was Jo Cooper.

"Coop! Boy, am I glad to see you! We need to get out of here, there are—"

"I know. After I found those Penguin Police Clowns ransacking my apartment, I got the heck out of there. I knew they would likely be tracking my car, but luckily, I just happened upon an ice-cream truck idling in a parking lot. Check it out!"

Just behind Cooper was a beat-up old truck with a giant fiberglass ice-cream cone affixed to the roof.

"It's like I died and went to heaven!" said Lucinni.

"You'll be going to the opposite if the penguins catch up to us," said Cooper. "Get in." She held open the door as Zengo, Lucinni, and Diaz piled into the back. But O'Malley stopped short.

"Don't even think about it, O'Malley. *I'm* driving," Cooper said.

O'Malley dropped his shoulders. He would never win this fight.

Cooper closed the door behind them and jumped into the driver's seat. She put the car into neutral and let the truck slowly roll out of the side parking lot just as the Penguin Police Force knocked down the door of Lucky Strike.

As soon as she hit the street, she punched the

engine, threw the engine into drive, and put the pedal to the floor. As the vehicle rushed through the city streets, Lucinni, Diaz, and O'Malley were already dipping their webbed hands into the Popsicle freezer.

"So what's the plan?" called Cooper. "I don't know how long we'll be able to drive around before we get pulled over by the Penguin Police Force. They're probably under orders to search every vehicle they come across."

"I've got a tape with evidence that could not only prove that Benny the Tusk isn't a threat, but could implicate Pandini in some serious crimes," said Zengo, patting the boom box. "If it's what we think it is, then the city could be in even more danger than we suspected. We've got to get it to the news media."

"But who can we trust?" asked O'Malley. "As far as I can tell, the mayor has everyone at the *Krier* and Action News tucked into his tuxedo pockets, just like the Penguin Police Force."

"We're taking this directly to Derek Dougherty," said Zengo as he held the tape aloft.

"WHAT?" everyone shouted in unison.

"We can't trust that slimy mudslinger any farther than we can throw him!" said O'Malley.

"Derek may seem like he's in Pandini's pocket," said Zengo. "But I have a feeling that, deep down, he has only one loyalty—to the story. If we have reliable evidence that Pandini has been playing the people of Kalamazoo City all the way to the mayor's office, he's going to be just as keen as we are. We're hand-delivering him the biggest story of his career!"

"I don't know about this, Zengo," said Cooper. "It's risky. We've only got one shot at deciding what to do with this tape."

"No, I think the kid is right," said O'Malley. "It's a much bigger risk NOT to get this tape to Derek. We don't have many options now, but he's the best we've got."

"Okay, but how are we going to get it to him?" asked Cooper. "There's no way we can get anywhere near the newspaper's offices without being spotted."

"We'll use a pay phone to call him and have him meet us somewhere safe," said O'Malley. He rummaged through his pockets and pulled out a few coins.

"Great!" said Zengo. "Now if we could only find a few dinosaurs to help us dial the numbers . . ."

"Can it, Zengo. There's a pay phone up at the gas station coming up on Sullivan Street. Hang a left,

172

Cooper." Jo Cooper obliged, and soon they were pulling into the parking lot at Happy's Petroleum. Sure enough, there was a decrepit pay phone just outside.

Zengo jumped out of the car carrying the boom box, picked up the receiver, and popped in the coins. He called Information and had them patch him through to the *Krier*'s offices, and from there he was transferred to Derek Dougherty's desk.

"Hello?" said a lazy voice at the other end of the line.

"Dougherty, this is Rick Zengo. I have something here that I think you'll find very interesting." He pressed Play on the boom box. A smooth voice filled the air.

"What do you suppose I would feeeeeel when I saw youuuu? My heart beats right outta my chest . . ." Zengo snatched the tape out of the boom box.

"Um, Zengo, are you asking me to slow dance? I don't have time for this nonsense."

"No, hold up! That was the wrong tape!" He fumbled to get the correct tape out of his back pocket and into the cassette player. He couldn't afford to lose Dougherty's attention. Zengo closed the deck and hit Play. Immediately, there was more talk of the illegal fish trade, followed by a phone conversation between Pandini and someone Zengo didn't know talking about sabotaging the Kalamazoo City Dome. *That narwhal hears everything*, he thought.

As the tape played, he glanced at the street, in case any Penguin Police Force cars were passing by. After a minute, he pressed Stop. "Derek, I know we've had our differences in the past, but you have to listen to me: everything you're hearing is from a tape in my possession, and there's more where that came from. This thing is filled with years' worth of illicit activity.

All the dirty things Pandini's done on his climb to the top. I think there's enough here to—"

The phone went dead. Zengo looked back at the pay phone to see a flipper on the receiver.

"Good afternoon, Mr. Zengo," said Sergeant Brayden Baghai. "I was hoping that I would be able to bring you in myself."

Zengo slid the boom box behind his back, but it was no use. The Penguin Police Force had him surrounded, and they all had their boomerangs drawn.

"I suggest you surrender peacefully," the sergeant continued. "First, why don't you hand over what you have behind your back?"

Zengo took a deep breath and slowly reached behind him to press Eject. He put the cassette in Baghai's flipper. The penguin considered it for a moment and then handed it to one of his detectives. "Take that back to the station. No one listens to it until I get back there, though. Got it?"

"Yessir."

"Now," Baghai continued, "let's see those webbed hands behind your head."

Zengo knew the drill all too well. He slowly raised his hands and placed them behind his head. He surveyed the parking lot; the ice-cream truck was parked off to the side, engine off, garnering none of the PPF's attention. O'Malley made a move to get out of the truck to help, but Zengo shook his head. It wouldn't do them any good for all of them to get caught.

Sergeant Baghai took out his walkie-talkie. "We got him. We're bringing him along now."

A PPF officer pulled Zengo's arms behind his back and handcuffed him. He led him to a cruiser and, before throwing him into the backseat, cracked him over the head with the butt of his boomerang. Zengo blacked out.

The cruisers drove off into the setting sunlight, their sirens blaring. Cooper, O'Malley, Lucinni, and Diaz watched in horror from the ice-cream truck.

"How did they find us?" asked Cooper aloud.

Then the answer came. A vibration noise from Diaz's back pocket. "Diaz?" she asked angrily.

Diaz took his phone out of his pocket and silenced it. "I-I-I-I'm sorry. I couldn't throw it in the garbage! I camped out overnight to be one of the first to sport the new gold-trimmed model."

Everyone looked like they wanted to throw Diaz in the garbage. Even Lucinni.

"Destroy it," said Cooper, her gaze more intense than any of them had ever seen. "Right now. You just got Zengo caught—who knows what they're going to do with him. We have to find him, and we can't let them get the drop on us again."

Diaz reluctantly put the phone on the floor of the cab and stepped on it, cracking it in half.

Cooper nodded curtly, then turned the key and stepped on the gas. The truck peeled out of the parking lot and out onto the streets, tailing the car ahead of them. "Hang on to something, boys. It's going to be a bumpy ride."

PANDINI HIGH-RISE CONSTRUCTION SITE, 6:12 P.M.

Rick Zengo came to with a terrible headache. His hands remained bound behind his back; the ropes were tight and cut into the skin beneath his fur. His stomach felt like it had been on a roller coaster, and all the blood was rushing to his head. He opened his eyes wide and realized that he was upside down. Blurry figures walked about around him, and behind them was the Kalamazoo City skyline. He remembered what Sergeant Baghai had said before he had been knocked out, about bringing him to Pandini. This must have been one of his new buildings under construction. All around him were partially built walls, exposed beams and pipes, and industrial equipment. He couldn't tell what floor he was on, but he knew he was up high.

There was the sound of an elevator door opening, and to his left, a splash of light spilled onto the unfinished wood floor. A shadowy figure was silhouetted in the doorway. Whoever it was stepped out of the elevator and approached Zengo.

"Lift him up higher," growled a voice that was all too familiar. Zengo felt his body get hoisted in the

air. "So you thought you would expose me using some ridiculous tape from that ancient fish, did you, Rick?"

"Game's not over yet, Frank," said Zengo defiantly. "You're a disgrace to this city, just like your father was."

"I see you've got a smart mouth on you. Bobby, could you help Zengo out with that, please?"

Pandini stepped aside and his bodyguard came forward with a bar of soap. "You need to clean up if you want to talk to Mr. Pandini." Bobby put the bar of soap in Zengo's mouth.

Zengo immediately spat it out. "I'm not the dirty one around here," he said.

"You know, Zengo," said Pandini as he took out an emery board to file his nails, "I've been working on my plan to take control of this city for some time now. Longer than you've been alive. Everyone thought my father was a criminal, but he wasn't. He was a hero. He took a city that didn't know what it was, and for a few glorious years, he turned it into a paradise for anyone who took what they wanted and apologized to no one. Unfortunately, not everyone saw things the way he did. But you know that—I suppose the roots of our family trees have been entangled for years now, haven't they?"

The elevator opened again, and five or six of Pandini's goons filed onto the floor to join Bobby. Pandini paced around Zengo as he continued to dangle from the ceiling. "I set out long ago to restore everything my father built. But I didn't make the same mistakes he did. I knew that criminals didn't need to hide in the shadows anymore—as long as a person appeared to follow the law, there was no limit to what he could take. And everything went just as planned. My businesses made me rich and ingratiated me with everyone in Kalamazoo City. With a name like Pandini, well, that was no easy task. But it taught me a valuable lesson: if you give people what they want and tell them what they want to hear, there's nothing they won't forgive and forget. The restaurants, the nightclubs, the cushy seats in the new sports stadiums that I built . . . Soon people stopped thinking of the name 'Frank Pandini' with fear and started thinking about it with respect, even affection."

Pandini stopped pacing right in front of the hanging platypus. He poked him with a single claw, and Zengo swung back and forth. "Then this new rookie detective

joins the Platypus Police Squad. Before long, he's
snooping around my businesses. He's shutting down
my carefully built illegal fish trade. Turns out he's the
grandson of the detective who worked so hard to bring
down my father so many years ago—yet another lousy
cop who is, for some reason, obsessed with this idea
that people need to obey the law, despite all evidence
to the contrary. And so I altered my plans, and Rick
my boy, you played along beautifully. I spearheaded
perhaps the most corrupt project in the history of
the city—the Kalamazoo City Dome—and set up the
mayor to take the fall when you inevitably exposed
it. I then planted enough evidence to frame my only

competition for the mayor's office, knowing you'd uncover all of it, and uncover it you did, handing me the election on a silver platter. Thank you for that, by the way."

Zengo seethed but remained quiet.

"At that point, I thought I was in the clear," Pandini continued. "I had the city in the palm of my hand, and there was only one job left: destroying the joke of an institution that had dragged my father's name through the mud before dragging him off to jail: the Platypus Police Squad. And that didn't just mean shutting you down—it meant embarrassing you publicly, tricking the very city you were created to protect into despising you. And thanks to my technology team—and their talents for creating cell phones that conveniently erase messages and appointments, security cameras and microphones that can easily be manipulated, and so much more—that proved to be a pretty simple job as well."

Zengo was finding it more and more difficult to keep quiet. O'Malley had been right about the phones from the beginning. It was all a trap.

Pandini stepped toward the view of the skyline and the huge body of water beyond. "Then another problem reared its ugly head: the narwhal. Benny the Tusk. Years ago, he stabbed my father in the back. Sent him down the river. Had more dirt on my family than a vacuum—he always was good at gathering secrets. He hadn't surfaced in years, but I had a feeling he'd be back one day. And when rumors began of a large shadow in the waters around Kalamazoo, I knew he had returned to take a shot at me, same as he did my dad. I couldn't have that. I tried to get you and your talented but clueless compatriots to help me out once again by putting that fish at the bottom of the ocean for good. The one time you darn detectives don't do your jobs . . . but no matter. Your ineptitude was enough for me to shoot down the PPS for good and install these trusty penguins in your place. Why penguins, you ask? Let's be honest: penguins are just way more popular with your average citizen than platypuses. Not to mention the fact that their cute and cuddly qualities meant that nobody would suspect that they were in my back pocket the whole time."

Zengo was speechless. This was all his fault. If only he'd been smarter, seen Pandini for what he was. . . . Now it was too late.

"Neither you nor those ridiculous penguins were able to catch Benny the Tusk, but in the end, it doesn't matter. The past shall remain buried. You got your hands on all the evidence he had on me, and I've got my hands on you. And just like that cassette tape is getting destroyed over at Penguin Police Force headquarters, I'm about to do the same to you."

Pandini moved to the corner of the floor, where a missing wall opened up to a sheer drop. "I'm afraid that your time is up, Detective Zengo. I hope that you've enjoyed this little chat. I've long known that, when it comes to you and your grandfather, the apple didn't fall far from the tree, as they say. Well, we're about to see just how far that apple can actually fall."

Pandini raised his paw to a lever on the wall and pulled. The chain holding Zengo lurched toward the ledge. Zengo squirmed against his bonds, but it was no use—he was trapped.

Pandini lifted his paw again to the lever beside the first one: the control to release the chain. But just as he was about to throw it, a boomerang knocked his paw away.

"Zengo's not going to fall as far as you think, Pandini," said Jo Cooper. Beside her, Corey O'Malley caught the boomerang he'd thrown on its return trip.

Pandini rolled his eyes. "Don't you platypuses ever give up?" He waved his paw at the intruders. "Boys, if you don't mind?"

Pandini's goons pulled out their boomerangs.

PANDINI HIGH-RISE CONSTRUCTION SITE, 6:44 P.M.

Cooper and O'Malley ducked behind a pillar as the boomerangs ricocheted off of the steel beams around them. O'Malley wiped his brow.

"What now?" he asked Cooper. He flinched at the sound of more boomerangs clanging against the metal pillar. The sounds got louder as Pandini's thugs drew closer.

"Don't worry, O'Malley. I have a plan." Cooper eyed an open fuse box on an adjacent wall. "Take cover." Cooper reached for a screwdriver left on the support beam, flipped it once, and then threw it like a knife toward the circuit breaker. Sparks flew, and the dangling safety lights went dark. Pandini moved to the elevator and pressed the button to summon it, but nothing happened—the power was out.

O'Malley and Cooper used the moment of distraction to make their move. They each jumped down, using one of Pandini's henchmen to cushion their fall, and kicked the criminals' boomerangs out of reach. Weaponless, but not finished, the henchmen lunged at the detectives. One of their fists connected with O'Malley's jaw, sending him sailing through the air and landing with a thud.

Cooper threw a quick uppercut that connected solidly with the other criminal's jaw and knocked him cold. She turned back toward O'Malley just as his attacker was about to smash a crowbar on his head.

But before she could do anything, O'Malley shot up, grabbed a fire extinguisher that had been lying near him, and blinded his attacker with a face full of foam. The attacker dropped the crowbar on his own foot and, shrieking with pain, grabbed at his eyes. O'Malley dropped the goon with one swing.

The two detectives spun around just in time to see Pandini escaping down a nearby stairwell with the last of his cronies.

"After him!" shouted O'Malley.

"We need to rescue Zengo first!" said Cooper.

The two of them rushed back across the floor to the ledge, but the chain hung empty. Instead, Pandini's bodyguard, Bobby, was silhouetted against the darkening sky, holding Zengo upside down, suspended over nothing but the drop.

"You actually think you can stop Pandini?" Bobby laughed. "He's been playing this city like a cheap piano for years."

"Freeze!" yelled Cooper.

The wind picked up and blew Zengo's tail aloft.

Bobby sneered. "A platypus has a bill like a bird . . . but can it fly like one?"

He opened his fist, and Rick Zengo felt the cool night air rushing against his fur.

PANDINI HIGH-RISE CONSTRUCTION SITE, 7:12 P.M.

As Rick Zengo fell, he was surprised to find he was calm. He was not scared; he was not in pain. Pandini had won, and soon everything would be over. He looked above him as O'Malley and Cooper rushed to the edge and watched him, helpless to do anything. He felt as if he were moving in slow motion.

Then the world suddenly shifted back to regular speed. He felt a fierce tug at his collar. Then a strong jerk. And then his body hit solid ground, and he tumbled across the floor.

Stunned, he struggled to get to his knees, right-side

up finally. He blinked several times to bring his eyes into focus. A vision of an unlikely ally came into focus before him.

"Y-you saved me?" Zengo managed to utter.

"I don't know what's the bigger story, Rick," said Derek Dougherty as he cut through the ropes that held Zengo's hands behind his back. "The one you called me about, or the fact that you and I seem to be on the same side for once. Now, what happened to the tape?"

Zengo smiled and laughed as he reached into his underwear. "It's right here!" He pulled out the tape, miraculously unharmed. "I was able to get it out of the boom box and stick it in my skivvies without the Penguin Police Force noticing! They think they have it—but they just confiscated a mixtape full of power ballads."

He made a move to hand the evidence over to the reporter, but before he could, it was snatched by a furry paw.

"Gentlemen, gentlemen," said Frank Pandini Jr., "how very disappointed I am to discover that you two are working together, after years of such useful strife." With a small movement of his giant paws, Pandini cracked the tape in two  pieces. He pulled out the tape ribbon and tossed it over his shoulder. It floated away on the night air. "That was very deceitful of you, young platypus."

"Mr. Mayor," said Derek, "I don't suppose I can get a comment on the evidence contained on that tape, or what you said to Detective Zengo on the floor above us, which altogether casts you in a very suspicious light?"

Pandini pinched Derek by the scruff of his neck and lifted him to eye level. "You shouldn't have come here, Derek. I've always liked you. So simpleminded, so easily manipulated. But if you're going to become yet another complication for me, it's not going to end well for you."

Derek swallowed loudly. "I suspected as much, Mr. Mayor. Which is why I decided to save some time and write my story before coming here. If I don't call my boss tonight, the story is set to run in the morning's paper."

Pandini growled. Clearly he would need to negotiate with the infuriating little lizard. "I'll deal with you in a moment," he said, tossing Derek aside like a banana peel. The panda yanked Zengo to his feet. "I was so hoping not to get my suit dirty tonight. But I'm afraid the old adage is true: if you want something done right, you have to do it yourself." Pandini reached his free paw back; his claws glistened in the moonlight. Derek gasped.

Zengo looked deep into Pandini's eyes. They were the eyes of Pandini Sr., the very eyes Zengo's grandfather once stared down without blinking. Now it was his turn.

Before Pandini could strike, Zengo head-butted his enemy right between those two tiny, cruel eyes. Pandini loosened his grip just long enough for Zengo to bust free. As Pandini regained his footing, Zengo put up his fists.

"It ends here, Pandini. This isn't your city, and it

never will be! I took a vow to protect it—badge or not! Let's go!"

Pandini rubbed his brow, but the scowl on his face remained. In a quick movement, the panda jumped into the air and pounced on the platypus. They both tumbled to the ground. Zengo kicked Pandini's hulking body off himself and was quick to get up. His body may have been bruised, but his spirit was not. Pandini staggered up and turned to meet Zengo's webbed fist connecting with his jaw. He fell to the ground.

Pandini stood up again, only to get tackled to the ground by Zengo. They rolled over and over, trading punches. Their tangled bodies inched closer and closer to the edge of the floor, still a hundred feet above the ground. To the side, Derek continued to hide his head in horror.

Zengo landed punch after punch, but the giant bear's hide was too strong. In a single motion Pandini grabbed the detective by the tail and flung him toward the edge. Zengo dug his claws into the floor and barely kept himself from flying off the ledge.

Pandini rushed him again, but the young platypus could still move fast. He dodged, and Pandini flew past him, tripping on a discarded board. As he fell, he reached out to break his fall, but then realized there was nothing to hold on to. He was right at the edge. Pandini teetered back into the night sky and twisted around, his eyes filled with terror. Zengo leaped forward. In that moment, he could have given Pandini the final shove to send him into oblivion.

Instead, Zengo reached his hand out and grabbed hold of Pandini's collar.

"Save me!" the panda pleaded. Zengo knew that if their positions had been swapped, Zengo would be flat as a pancake right now. But he wasn't Pandini. He was Lieutenant Dailey's grandson. He pulled Pandini back into the building and slammed him to the ground.

Pandini lay on the floor, still shaking with fear. "You saved my life," he said.

"I'm a member of the Platypus Police Squad—that's what I do." Zengo stepped on Pandini's back and pulled his arms back. He pulled a set of handcuffs from his back pocket and slapped them on Pandini's wrists. "I do this too. You may have confiscated my badge and my boomerang, but luckily I held on to my cuffs."

Derek finally climbed to his feet as Zengo stood, his foot still on the limp bear's back.

"Did you really write your story already?" Zengo asked.

"No," said Derek. "I was bluffing. Besides, what you played for me wasn't exactly enough for a front-page

piece. But what I saw and recorded tonight was." He took his phone out of his pocket and held it up.

"And now that their boss has been captured, I'm sure his hired muscle will be more than happy to sell their old boss down the river," said Cooper as she and O'Malley made their way onto the floor, each of them with two struggling henchmen in tow. "Isn't that right, boys?"

"They'd never!" growled Pandini.

"What do you think, Bobby?" said Cooper, shaking the hippo. "Would you rather have an all-expenses-paid trip to the slammer with your boss here, or a no-expenses-paid trip back to wherever you came from with your record clear?"

"Neither one, actually," said Bobby. He leaned into the walkie-talkie on his shoulder. "Sergeant Baghai! Now!"

Everybody turned as the deafening sound of a helicopter came up quickly, and they covered their eyes as a blinding light shot through the floor. The chopper turned slightly, and emblazoned on the side was the logo for the Penguin Police Force.

"Everybody freeze!" said a voice over the bullhorn. "You're under arrest! Let's see your hands in the air!"

Zengo's eyes fell. This, after everything else that had gone down. He slowly raised his hands. O'Malley and Cooper did the same, as did Derek. The platy-puses' fur tussled in the wind that blew in from the circulating blades. From the floor, Pandini sneered.

"Now," came the voice again, "put your left foot for-ward."

Zengo, Cooper, and O'Malley looked at each other, befuddled.

"You heard me! Put your left foot in!"

They each put their left foot forward.

"Now—put your left foot out."

They did that too. What was going on?

"Now put your left foot in and shake it all about!"

Lucinni and Diaz stuck their heads out of the window of the helicopter. "That's right, do the hokey-pokey, O'Malley!" yelled Lucinni.

"Ha-ha! You should have seen the looks on your

faces. *That's* what it's all about!" shouted Diaz. The two clowns high-fived. "Told you we were the good guys, Baghai."

Sergeant Brayden Baghai popped his head out the window too. "Let's just hope you have the evidence we need. Bring this bird down to the ground, boys."

PANDINI HIGH-RISE CONSTRUCTION SITE, 7:57 P.M.

Zengo had never been so happy to stand on solid ground. At the foot of the half-constructed building, Derek played the audio recorded on his phone for Sergeant Baghai.

"This sounds like exactly what we were looking for," said the new police chief. "I'll have to talk to the district attorney, but I'm thinking this is enough to lock Frank Pandini Jr. away for a long, long time. The only daylight he'll see will be during the yard work he'll be doing in federal prison."

Sergeant Baghai turned to the platypuses. They

209

had all seen better days. Their bodies were bruised, and while they had brought Frank Pandini to justice, their heads still hung low. They weren't cops anymore, after all.

Sergeant Baghai waddled up to them. "You have all served Kalamazoo City bravely. Even after you thought you were dismissed from the police force, you followed the case through to the end."

"Thought?" said Zengo.

"The Penguin Police Force was never going to replace the Platypus Police Squad," said Sergeant Baghai. "Even if Pandini thought it would. That's because there is no Penguin Police Force. We're federal agents. When the things happening in Kalamazoo City came to our attention—the government corruption, the possible return of a fugitive narwhal—we went undercover as a team of police-for-hire to see if we couldn't get to the bottom of what was going on. I wanted you in Penguin Police Force custody to protect you! We had just uncovered enough about Pandini's ultimate goal to know that you were a part of it. We gave you that knockout shot to make sure we could get you away without any problems—as you likely know by now, Pandini has cameras everywhere. But before I could get you back to the station, Pandini's goons arrived to claim you. We couldn't stop them without breaking our cover, and so we decided to follow them. But we had no idea what he was planning on doing to you. You almost lost your life up there. I'm sorry, Detective—"

Baghai's words were interrupted by the sound of Pandini growling as he and his crew were thrown into

the backseats of police cruisers. The Penguin Police Force logo, which was emblazoned on the side of the car, was ripped off by the attending penguin to reveal the Platypus Police Squad logo underneath.

"These cars are all yours," he said. "But the prisoners? After you drive us to our paddy wagon on the Kalamazoo City border, we'll be taking them to a federal prison. We have a few questions for them as they wait to face trial."

"After all, you are back on the job," added Baghai.

Zengo, O'Malley, and Cooper all breathed a huge sigh of relief.

"But what about Sergeant Plazinski?" asked Zengo. "Is he back on the job? Come to think of it, I haven't heard from him since the PPS was shut down."

"You haven't heard from him because he's been relaxing on a small Caribbean island," said Baghai.

"What?" said O'Malley and Zengo together.

"How could the sergeant afford that?" Cooper added.

"Quite easily, it turns out," said Baghai. "It wasn't long after Pandini shut down the PPS and called us in that we followed a suspicious line of money that led from Pandini right to Plazinski. The sergeant had been taking bribes from Pandini for years. He took off for a long vacation as soon as he was 'let go.' We couldn't pick him up before without arousing suspicion, but don't worry: now that Pandini has been captured, he's next on our list."

Zengo was speechless. Plazinski was crooked! It was almost too much to believe.

"So I guess the PPS will need a new sergeant?" said O'Malley.

"Dude!" said Zengo. "Do you really think you're

213

sergeant material? At your age?"

"I'm going to try not to be offended by that," O'Malley replied. "And to answer your question, no, I wasn't thinking of me. I was thinking of Cooper."

Cooper smiled. "Me? Really?"

"You bet," said O'Malley. "You were running the squad better than Plazinski by the end anyway. I've seen more than a few sergeants in my time, and I know you've got what it takes."

If Jo Cooper were the sort of platypus who blushed, she would have right then.

"I'll even write you a letter of recommendation," O'Malley continued. "On one condition."

"What's that?"

"You make sure Zengo and I stay partners." O'Malley smiled at the young detective.

It was Zengo's turn to blush.

"If you're going to be the new sergeant, I guess you'll be needing these," said Diaz, handing Cooper a keyring.

"What are these?" she asked.

"Keys to all the squad vehicles," said Lucinni. "We, um . . . took a few souvenirs when we were all let go."

"So *that's* how you got your hands on that helicopter," said Baghai. "That is highly illegal."

"Hey, we pretty much saved the day, didn't we?" Diaz said. "DIAZ AND LUCINNI REPRESENT!"

After the crowd finally dispersed, the paperwork was complete, and Cooper had left with Baghai to put Pandini and his crew into federal custody, O'Malley drove Zengo back home. The roads were silent for once, and bathed in light from the streetlamps.

"Let's pull over to the docks for a second," said Zengo. "I want to take a look at that moon Vanessa and her boyfriend were talking about."

"Don't you just want to get some sleep?" asked O'Malley with a yawn.

"I do. After that."

O'Malley sighed and turned the steering wheel. "Fine. But if the Frank's Franks stand is open, I'm getting a late-night snack."

O'Malley pulled the car up to the edge of the docks. The moon hung in the sky over the water. It was a magnificent evening. But as Zengo had hoped, he saw something even more magnificent. Benny, free at last from the past that had hounded him for years, jumped out of the water, let out a big narwhalian wail, and splashed back down into the ocean. Zengo nodded his head.

O'Malley put his hand on Zengo's shoulder. "You've done good, kid," he said. "Your grandfather would be proud. I know I am."

Zengo smiled.

CHAPTER

22

**PLATYPUS POLICE SQUAD HEADQUARTERS,
8:03 A.M.
ONE MONTH LATER**

"Lucinni, sit up in your chair!" barked Sergeant Cooper.

The detective nearly fell over as he rushed to correct his posture. Sergeant Cooper stood behind her desk. She was tough, but she ran a tight ship.

"As I was saying, Detectives," said Cooper. "After the ceremony today, I want you all back here in the station for a squadwide briefing. A ring of petty thieves has been striking the Kalamazoo City Mall.

219

We're going to need to go undercover to infiltrate these young punks."

"I volunteer to go undercover in the food court!" said O'Malley.

"The mall's been hit hard enough by these thefts," said the sergeant. "They don't need to have cinnamon buns going missing on top of it."

"Oh, come on," said O'Malley.

"All right. You can go as a food court employee, but only because this is your last case!"

"Last case?" asked Zengo. "What, are you going on vacation or something?"

Cooper and O'Malley exchanged glances. "I thought you told him," she said.

"Uh, I've been trying to, Sergeant," said O'Malley. He looked at Zengo, who was searching O'Malley's face for answers. "Guess the cat is out of the bag." He shrugged his shoulders. "I'm retiring, kid."

Zengo's bill dropped. "No, you're not, O'Malley. We still have a lot of work to do."

"I'm old, kid. Pandini is behind bars. It's time."

"But," said Zengo, sputtering, "there always needs to be an O'Malley on the force!"

"Oh, there will be," he said.

At that moment, Vanessa O'Malley walked into the sergeant's office. "Hi, Dad. Heading over to my first day at the academy, but Mom wanted me to stop by because you forgot your blueberry muffin this morning." She dropped a bag in O'Malley's lap, kissed his cheek, and turned to leave. "Hey, Rick," she said over her shoulder as she closed the door behind her.

Zengo raised his eyebrows.

"It wasn't my idea," said O'Malley. "But sometimes you have to let the kids leave the nest. Speaking of which, I'm planning on spending a lot more time at home with the ones I have who are still there. Karen already has plans to go back to work outside the home.

She put everything on hold for my career, and now she's getting back to hers. These old bones of mine—they can't handle any more foot chases or any more tackling the scum of the city. . . . I'm tired, Zengo."

"You can debate the pros and cons of O'Malley's retirement on your own time, boys," interrupted Sergeant Cooper. "Mayor McGovern is expecting us at City Hall within the hour." Cooper threw Zengo a tie. "It's a clip-on, Rick. I'm sure you can handle it."

"I know how to put on a tie," Zengo grumbled. He didn't even mind wearing one today; after all, it wasn't every day that you received the key to the city.

"I want you all in your formal uniforms and outside the building by 12:30. And you know what I consider on time. . . ."

"Ten minutes early," everyone said in unison.

A smile spread across Cooper's bill. "I knew I'd be able to whip this team into shape. Let's go!"

Cooper opened her office door to find Peggy about to knock.

"There's been . . . a report . . . of another robbery. Shoplifters hit the . . . Slushie Haven in the mall's . . . food . . . court."

Cooper looked at O'Malley and Zengo. "Pack your

uniforms and head to the mall. But don't put them on until *after* you've investigated the Slushie Haven. I don't want you showing up covered in purple gunk."

"What are we, children?" demanded O'Malley.

Cooper held up O'Malley's tie. "This tie was clean when you walked into my office."

"I feel that the blueberry stain adds a certain symmetry to the pattern," he said.

O'Malley and Zengo darted off to their unmarked squad car, parked in the station lot. They opened the back doors and hung their freshly pressed uniforms. O'Malley stopped short of stepping into the driver's seat.

Zengo held his door open as well. "What's up?"

O'Malley took the keys out of his pocket and threw them across to Zengo, who caught them.

"Your turn." O'Malley walked around the car to the passenger side. "You heard me, kid. You drive this time."

Zengo closed O'Malley's car door and clutched the car keys in his webbed fist.

"All right!" Zengo slid across the hood and hopped in the driver's seat, closing the door and revving the engine. They both clicked their seat belts, and

223

Zengo peeled out of the driveway, hip-hop already pounding out of the speakers.

"Rule number one, retiree: nobody touches this radio but me, got it?"

"Don't push it, kid."

12

ACKNOWLEDGMENTS

Thank you to the amazing teams at HarperCollins and Walden Pond Press for making the Platypus Police Squad a reality! You all are superb! Thank you, too, to Rebecca Sherman and Eddie Gamarra for their guidance.

Thank you to my real-world cop friends Corey McGrath and Chris Zengo. Love to the 1998 Yellow Platypus at the Hole in the Wall Gang Camp. Thank you to Joey Weiser and Michele Chidester for their help in shading this book, and to Austin Gifford for his assistance in my studio.

And love and thanks for the eternal support and patience of Gina, Zoe, and Lucy Krosoczka as I completed this book. And Ralph and Frank—thank you for the pug snores.

JARRETT J. KROSOCZKA

is the author and illustrator of the Lunch Lady graphic novel series, a two-time winner of the Children's Choice Book Award, as well as many picture books. He can be heard on "The Book Report with JJK," his radio segment on SiriusXM's Kids Place Live. Jarrett lives in Northampton, Massachusetts, with his wife, two daughters, and their pug, Ralph Macchio. You can visit him online at www.studiojjk.com.

Also available as an ebook.

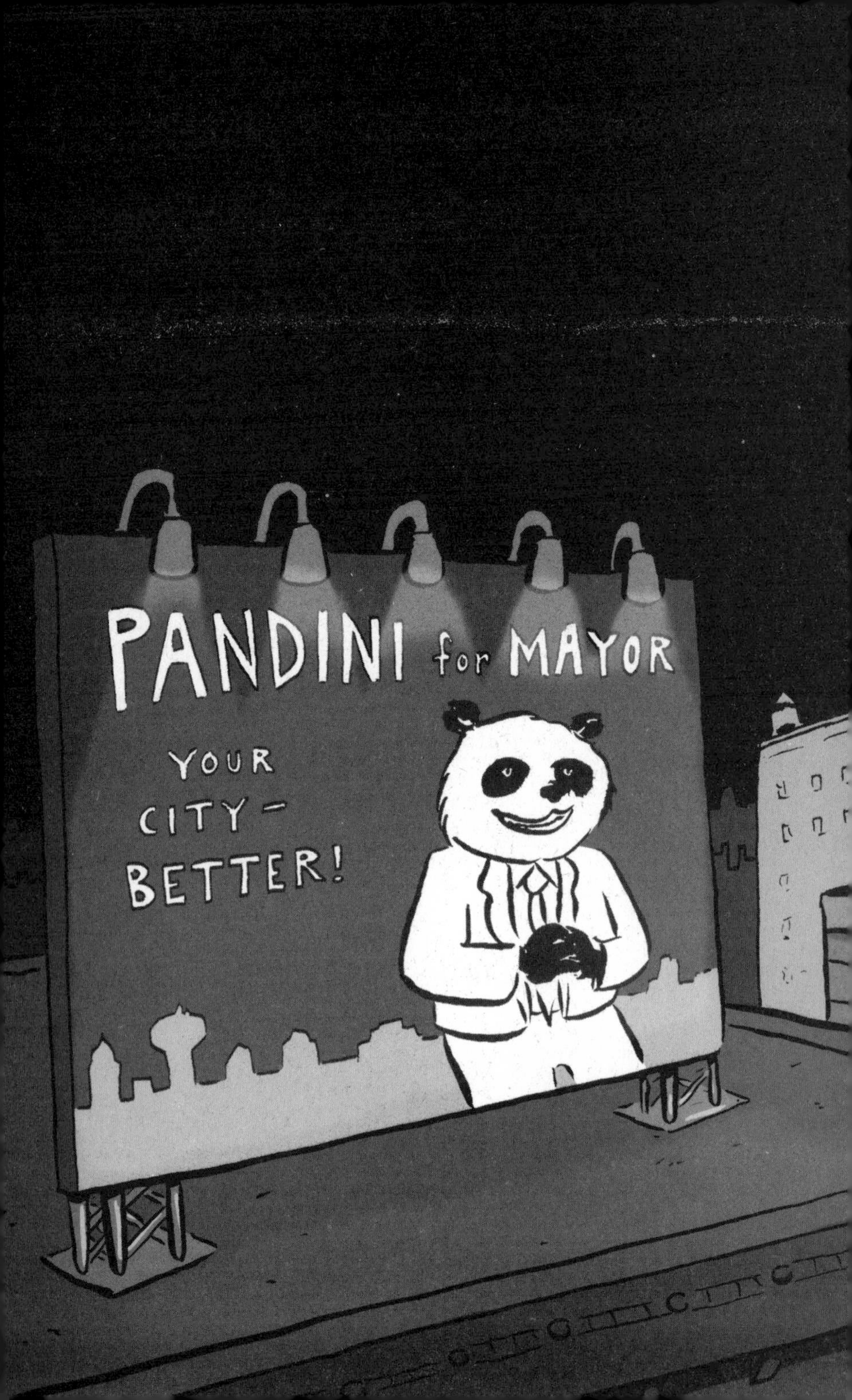
PANDINI for MAYOR
YOUR CITY– BETTER!

When trouble brews in Kalamazoo City, detectives ZENGO and O'MALLEY are on the case.

Book 1

Book 2

Book 3

Book 4

Read all the Platypus Police Squad books from JARRETT J. KROSOCZKA.

WALDEN POND PRESS
An Imprint of HarperCollinsPublishers

www.walden.com/books • www.harpercollinschildrens.com